FANTAIL BOOKS

She had to get out . . .

Jan fell forward through the open doorway, landing hard on her knees inside the fire-filled kitchen. For a moment she knelt there, her temples pounding. Then she reached around and felt the back of her head gingerly. There was a wetness she was sure could only be blood.

An intense flare of heat washed over her as a ceiling panel sagged near her, melting plastic dripping in long globs that burst into flame as they fell. She had to get out. An acrid odor of burning hair was added to all the other smells, and she knew her own curls were smoldering.

Kate Daniel

SWEET DREAMS

FANTAIL

FANTAIL BOOKS

Published by the Penguin Group
Penguin Books Ltd, 27 Wrights Lane, London W8 5TZ, England
Penguin Books USA Inc., 375 Hudson Street, New York, New York 10014, USA
Penguin Books Australia Ltd, Ringwood, Victoria, Australia
Penguin Books Canada Ltd, 10 Alcorn Avenue, Toronto, Ontario, Canada M4V 3B2
Penguin Books (NZ) Ltd, 182–190 Wairau Road, Auckland 10, New Zealand

Penguin Books Ltd, Registered Offices: Harmondsworth, Middlesex, England

First published in the United States of America by HarperCollins 1992
First published in Great Britain by Fantail 1993
10 9 8 7 6 5 4 3 2 1

Printed in England by Clays Ltd, St Ives plc
Set in Times

To Judith Tarr

For friendship, for encouragement—
for Judy

ONE

The smell was one she knew, but the name of it slipped from her mind like a wisp of vapor. It was growing stronger, along with her fear. Silence filled the night and rang in her ears. She pulled her robe tight against the cold as she walked across the bedroom.

She faced the door, her throat caught on the strange taste in the air. As she stretched out her hand to turn the knob, silence screamed a warning. She pushed the door open anyway.

A wall of flames fell on her, engulfing her hand and the doorknob. Her arm burned like a dry branch, while the smoke twisted around her in choking coils and her own screams filled the night.

* * *

1

The damp chill of a spring night caught her, and Janelle Scott shivered violently. She saw a pile of burning rubbish in the street and quickly pulled the front door closed. The smell of smoke must have triggered the nightmare. Tomorrow was trash pickup, and Aunt Leah had thrown out a number of cardboard boxes. Someone must have tossed a lit cigarette out a car window. Jan shivered again, then headed up to her bedroom. In the dining room the old clock struck two; outside, the streets were silent. No one drove down quiet residential streets at this hour, starting accidental fires. Jan reached the landing and looked out. The fire was burning down, and cardboard ash drifted in the light breeze.

She hurried into bed and pulled the down comforter up almost over her head. The sheets were cold against her feet, but gradually her own body heat warmed them. It had happened again. As far back as she could remember, Jan had walked in her sleep when she was upset. She'd sleepwalked almost nightly after the fire that had destroyed her home and killed her parents six months earlier. With the passing of time, the disturbing episodes had stopped. But within the past few weeks, they'd started again,

2

along with nightmares. Living through the fire had been bad. Reliving it endlessly in her dreams was almost unbearable.

Jan tried to relax into the warmth of the bed. She had to get back to sleep; tomorrow was a school day. But the nightmare was still vivid in her mind. The wall of fire had been real, and remembering it made the scars on her arm itch under the tight sleeve of her plain nightgown. Back then she'd had a beautiful robe with deep ruffles and lace on the sleeves. The ruffles had caught fire when she'd opened the door. She always wore long sleeves now to hide the ugly scars. But never any ruffles.

At last the quiet darkness soothed her, and she went back to sleep. As her thoughts faded into the half world of dreams, the smell of smoke tickled at her nostrils once more.

The alarm blared for a few minutes before Jan roused herself to turn it off. She hurried through her shower, then pulled on a pair of faded jeans and a bulky sweater. She ran a comb through her hair, all the attention she needed to give it these days. Half of her hair had been singed off in the fire. After she'd gotten out of the hospital, she'd had what was left cut short to match. The soft red curls she wore these days took almost no work, which helped when she was late.

Traces of nightmare lingered in her mind. The tragedy that had taken her family had left so many unanswered questions. Maybe that was why she couldn't shake the dreams. The cause of the blaze had never been determined. Even in dreams, Jan's memory couldn't fill the gap between her robe catching fire and the moment when the paramedics had found her on the lawn, burned and hysterical, the only survivor.

Grabbing her book bag, she hurried down the stairs to the kitchen. The rest of her new family was already eating. Uncle Peter, her father's younger brother, was spreading honey on a piece of toast. He looked a lot like her dad, and Jan felt a pang each time she looked at him.

Jan didn't know her uncle that well; he was always working, running the family business. Aunt Leah ruled the household. Jan slid into her seat as her aunt greeted her.

"Janelle, dear, you're late." Aunt Leah had a habit of stating the obvious. As always, she was perfectly dressed, her fluffy dark hair combed precisely. Jan gulped down her orange juice, then started on her oatmeal, wishing for the bacon and eggs her mother used to fix.

"Sorry," Jan said, "I overslept." Even after her shower, she still felt tired and sleepy. Too many interrupted nights. She wanted a cup of coffee, but Aunt Leah never had anything but decaf in the house. Maybe she could pick up a cup on the way to school. She needed something to help her wake up.

"That's, what, the third time in two weeks?" Jan's cousin Andrea shook her head. "You should sleep a little instead of working on your computer all night. C'mon, we'd better get going or we'll be late for first hour."

As Jan rushed through the rest of her breakfast, she wondered what Andrea had meant. Jan hadn't been up late, she just *felt* as though she'd been up half the night.

"You really should get to bed earlier on school nights, dear," Aunt Leah said. "You've got bags under your eyes. Maybe you need more vitamins."

Jan sighed. Aunt Leah was a great believer in vitamins and weird-tasting "health" foods, but Jan hated them. "I'm fine, Aunt Leah, but I'm late. See you after school." Andrea was waiting impatiently by the door. Jan bent over and kissed her aunt on the cheek, catching the faint scent of face powder.

Andrea said, "Come *on*, Jan!" She went out the door without waiting for a reply, and Jan grabbed her bag, running after her cousin. Fortunately the school was only a few blocks away. The two girls stretched their legs, shifting to a jog after a few paces. They didn't talk, saving their breath for speed. Jan's long legs made it easier for her; at five feet seven, she was several inches taller than Andrea. Even though they were first cousins, they didn't look a bit alike. Jan looked like her father and Uncle Peter, with bright red hair and cinnamon-colored eyes. Andrea took after Aunt Leah, petite and dark-haired.

After a block Andrea said, "If I wanted to run, I'd have gone out for the track team. You go on if you want to." She dropped back to a fast walk.

"We'll make it, I think," Jan said. The school was in sight now, and there were still students outside on the steps. The bell hadn't rung yet. "I'm too tired to run, anyway."

Andrea snorted. "Like I said, try sleeping."

"It seems like I can't get *enough* sleep lately." As Jan spoke, the warning bell sounded.

They hurried toward the building as the students on the step vanished through the door.

"It's your own fault," Andrea said. "Lately it seems like you're always up typing away on your computer. I hear you in the middle of the night." They reached the bottom of the steps and went up two at a time. "I know you like to write, but I'd like to get some sleep myself. Your light keeps waking me up." At the entrance Andrea ran off down the corridor to the left, calling over her shoulder, "See you third hour."

Jan turned right. Andrea was exaggerating, of course; Jan didn't stay up that late. Andrea had never understood Jan's love of writing. Just as she didn't understand why Jan preferred to work on the school newspaper and yearbook instead of joining the pep club and student council. This was Andrea's third year on the council, but Jan wasn't interested in politics. Not even school politics.

She reached English class and slid into her seat just as the tardy bell rang. Mike Greenly had the seat in front of her. Jan and Mike had been going together for over two years. As she sat down, he turned to say hi. "I wondered if you were going to be late again," he said. His smile faded as he looked at her. Jan knew how tired she must look. "More bad dreams?"

She nodded. She hadn't mentioned the nightmares to anyone but him. Before she could say anything, Mr. Buehler cleared his throat loudly. He was one of Jan's favorite teachers, but he was strict in class.

"Talk to you after class," Mike whispered as he turned back to face the chalkboard.

Mr. Buehler started to speak. Jan barely heard him. She stared at the back of Mike's head, wishing she didn't have to bother with school. Before this year she'd been a top student. Since the fire, though, her interest in school and almost everything but Mike and her writing had died. Jan felt as if Mike were the only one left who shared her interests; she knew him much better than she'd ever known Uncle Peter and Aunt Leah. Moving in with them had been almost like moving in with strangers.

The English class dragged on. When the bell finally rang, Jan realized that she'd barely listened to a word and had no idea of what the assignment was. She headed for the door with Mike, making a mental promise to make up the work later.

* * *

Jan ate lunch with Mike in the newspaper room. They had a lot in common, especially their love of writing and books. Mike had noticed that she'd checked out many of the same books that he had from the library. One day he'd left her a note at the checkout desk. He wanted to meet the girl whose reading tastes were as wide-ranging as his own.

Mike had encouraged Jan to write and talked her into joining the paper, which he edited. Now she had her own column covering community events, new movies, and things to do in Kenowa. It was one of the most popular features of the paper. They spent most noon hours talking and working together on the *Cat Claws*.

The lunch session with Mike was the high point of Jan's day. Afterward she felt sleepy and grouchy. She spent the day yawning. It wasn't the first time. Ever since she'd started sleepwalking again, she'd been walking around in a fog. If it continued much longer, she'd have to see a doctor, and that would mean a hassle with her aunt. Aunt Leah didn't believe in doctors, preferring her herbal remedies.

By bedtime Jan's head was pounding. She checked the medicine cabinet in the bathroom she shared with Andrea. She'd seen some aspirin in there the week before. Unfortunately, there was nothing there now except deodorant and toothpaste and makeup.

She knocked on the connecting door to Andrea's bedroom. "Andrea? You still up?" At her cousin's muffled response, she pushed the door open.

Andrea's bedroom was twice as large as Jan's, which had been the spare room until she moved in. Andrea was sitting up in the four-poster bed, working on homework. Jan felt a twinge of guilt; she hadn't done her trig yet. But she'd never be able to concentrate on sines and cosines with this headache.

Andrea looked up from the page. "Done your math yet?"

"No," Jan said. A yawn surprised her. "And I may not do it at all. My head's killing me. Do you have any aspirin?"

"Sorry, I used the last one the other day. These aren't aspirin, but they should help." Andrea slipped her feet into fuzzy blue slippers and went over to her purse. After a moment's rummaging, she came up with a pair of tablets. "They're ibuprofen."

"I don't care what they are, as long as they

work," Jan said. She went back to the bathroom for water to wash the pills down, then stepped back into Andrea's room. "How hard's the assignment?" She and Andrea were in the same math class.

"It's not that hard, it's just long. I've been working on it forever, almost. 'Fraid you won't be able to get to bed early tonight." Andrea grinned. "Not with this assignment."

"Well, I think I'll go to bed anyway," Jan said. Another yawn interrupted her. "Maybe I can finish it at lunch tomorrow."

"Yeah, sure." There was a flash of concern on Andrea's face as she added, "You do need some sleep. One incomplete isn't going to hurt your grade that much."

Won't hurt it any worse, you mean, Jan thought. Her grades had slipped badly this year, but she didn't care any longer. She said good night, went back into her room, and got immediately into bed. She didn't even glance at her math book.

Sometime during the night, Jan woke up, her heart pounding. She'd had another nightmare, but she couldn't remember any of it. There was a draft in the room. Jan wondered if she'd left the window open, but she was too drowsy to get

11

up and check. In the dim light that filtered through the curtains from the corner street-lamp, Jan could see the outlines of the room. Her room. This drafty corner bedroom, with the bare wood floors and single small bookshelf, wasn't her room and never really would be. She burrowed deeper into the covers, re-creating in her mind the comfortable, shabby room that she now saw only in dreams. Jan drifted back to sleep, picturing the faded hooked rug and crowded bookshelves that decorated her old bedroom.

In the morning Jan's headache was gone, but there was a heavy feeling in her head that was almost as bad. A shower cleared it somewhat, and by the time she and Andrea reached school, she felt almost normal again.

As they entered the building, Jan heard someone call. "Andrea! Did you guys see it last night?" Barb, the photographer from the *Cat Claws*, hurried over to join them.

"See what?" Andrea asked. Barb started to pull her aside, then shrugged. With a glance at Jan, she said, "The fire. You know the old Foote mansion near your house? It caught fire last night and almost burned to the ground. The news this morning said it was arson."

"Arson?" Andrea asked. "That's silly, why would anyone burn down that place? Nobody really even owns it."

"Maybe not," Barb said. "But it wasn't an accident." She glanced at Jan again and added, "I've got to get to class."

"Man, I can't believe that place is gone," Andrea said as they walked down the hall. "I wonder who did it. Remember the time we got inside?" They stopped by Jan's locker.

"I remember," Jan answered shortly, opening the locker door. She didn't want to think about fires or arson. There'd been some talk of arson six months earlier when her house had burned down, but without suspects or a motive, the talk had died. There probably never would be any definite answers. All Jan had was nightmares and questions. The worst ones were about the smoke detector. The alarm hadn't sounded, and her parents had died in their sleep. Jan tortured herself endlessly with the idea that she might have been able to save them if she'd awakened in time. But she'd never know.

When Jan got home that afternoon, the house was empty. Andrea had a student council meeting, and it was Aunt Leah's day for art class. Jan was glad to have the place to herself. Aunt Leah always fussed so much. And she kept making Jan drink those gross herbal teas that were supposed to be good for you. Jan thought they might cure diseases; they certainly tasted like medicine.

Usually the only snack in the house was those weird oat-bran cookies that tasted like straw. Since Jan knew Aunt Leah was going to be out, she'd picked up corn chips and a soda on the way home from school. For once she'd have a nice unhealthy snack. Jan sprawled on the couch in the family room, watching TV and munching happily. After a while she glanced at the clock. Over an hour had passed; Aunt Leah would be home any minute. Jan took the empty soda can out to the trash and pushed it under some paper. Then she went up to her room to get started on her term paper for economics. She had only two days until the rough draft was due. Before long she hit a snag. The information she needed wasn't in the books she had there; she'd have to go to the library. Jan got her sweater and book bag and left a note for her aunt. It was still an hour before sunset, and it was a nice evening for a walk.

The direct route led past the Foote place and Jan's old house. She never went that way anymore, preferring to avoid the empty lot that had been "home." Instead she took a parallel street. Buds were swelling on the trees, and all the early flowers were out. Jan focused on the feeling of spring in the air and didn't look toward the gap in the line of roofs two blocks away.

The library was a familiar haven, and she found the information she needed with little trouble. After working for forty-five minutes, she decided she'd had enough. She'd make a fast check for interesting books and then head back. She wandered up and down, picking up books as they caught her eye.

Suddenly she stopped. She was in front of a shelf of psychology books, and there was one that dealt with sleepwalking. She took it down and curiously leafed through it. Unfortunately, the book was aimed at doctors and psychology students. Jan had a good vocabulary, but she couldn't follow more than one word in five. She slid it back into place.

"Checking to see if you're crazy?" Andrea's voice behind her startled Jan so much that she knocked several books off the shelf. They both bent down to pick them up. Andrea went on, "I could tell you, if you want me to." She straightened up and looked at the book in her hands. *"The Subjective Experience of Somnambulism . . .* come on, Jan, what *is* this?"

"That's not the one I was looking at," Jan mumbled as she straightened the books. "I was just curious about some of these, but I couldn't read them."

Andrea looked over the titles and snorted. "No joke."

"What are you doing here?" Jan knew that sounded rude, but she wanted to get Andrea away from this section.

Andrea didn't take offense. "I have to get a book for English class. Book reports."

"I'm done with my work." Jan started to gather her books and notes. "You ready to leave?"

Andrea shook her head. "I just got here a few minutes ago. You go on, I'll see you later."

The sun had set by now, and streetlights were coming on as Jan left the library. She thought that maybe she'd come back next week and check out that book Andrea had picked up. Jan had talked to her family doctor about sleepwalking a couple of times, back after the fire. She didn't want to make a big deal out of it, but it was scary, waking up and finding herself in a strange place, with no memory of how she'd gotten there.

Her mind busy with memories and questions, Jan didn't realize where she was. Unconsciously, she had taken an old and familiar route. An acrid smell of dead smoke filled her nostrils, and Jan looked up. . . .

She was choking and her eyes were streaming as the smoke fastened like gray hands around her throat. Her arm screamed pain at her, burning—not just the ruffles and lace but the flesh itself. The quilt her grandmother had made was thrown across the foot of her bed, and she snatched it up, trying to wrap herself in the blanket. Grandmother's quilt—no, she couldn't use it, she couldn't ruin Grandmother's quilt. But her arm hurt, and the fire would eat the quilt anyway. Eat the quilt as it was eating her, as it was eating her life. Fires were hungry things.

Grandmother's quilt stank as she smothered the fire engulfing her arm. There was nothing left but pain and the taste of smoke. And the roar of the living fire. She stood there, wrapped in a smoldering blanket, listening.

The only sounds were the greedy fire and the sirens wailing around the dying house.

Jan tripped, books flying everywhere. She landed on her knees, breath knocked from her by the sudden fall. She was walking home from the library and . . . Jan froze, halfway back to her feet, as she looked up at the building in front of her.

She had tripped on the front steps. Inside, she could hear her uncle calling something to Aunt Leah. With shaking hands, Jan gathered the books, then stumbled up the stairs. She was back at the house.

And she had no idea how she'd gotten there.

TWO

Jan tried to pay attention in class the next morning. She couldn't, though; the events of the night before kept racing through her mind. Sleepwalking was one thing. She didn't like it, but she was used to it. But nothing like this had ever happened to her before. She had smelled the smoke and realized she was at the Footes' place, and then . . .

And then she'd found herself several blocks away. She must have fallen asleep or had a waking nightmare. Her mind had played a lot of tricks on her recently, but this was the scariest one yet. What was *wrong* with her?

School, for one thing, she decided. Everyone was talking about the fire. Since everyone knew what had happened to her family, very few people wanted to mention the word "fire" in front of Jan. Most of the conversations died when she approached. But another word was being used almost as much: arson.

At lunchtime the entire staff of the *Cat Claws* was gathered in the newspaper room. The paper came out on Thursdays, and every Wednesday there was a last-minute rush to complete it on time. Halfway through the lunch hour, Mr. Buehler walked in, grinning broadly. He was faculty adviser for the paper as well as Jan's English teacher. "Just picked up some mail addressed to the editor of the Kenowa Central High School *Cat Claws*," he announced. He tossed a large manila envelope to Mike.

Mike opened the envelope, then let out a yell loud enough to be heard out on the football field. "We did it!" He waved a letter overhead. "Best Class B paper in the state!" The Illinois Association of School Newspapers gave annual awards for excellence. This was the first time that Central had won.

Lunch turned into a party. Everyone on the staff had helped earn the award, but Mike had done the real work. Besides staying after school most days to edit articles and lay out the paper, Mike had organized fund-raisers to buy new equipment for the *Cat Claws*. Jan knew how much he cared about the paper, and she was happy for him—and a little proud.

They were so busy celebrating that when the bell rang for fifth hour, they still hadn't finished. The entire front page needed to be rewritten, since the award was now their lead story. Mike told everyone to show up after school for a work session; then there was a mad dash as everyone tried to get to their next class before the bell.

Jan was tardy to economics, which meant another detention—her third this month. Economics was Jan's least favorite class. At least they were working on their term papers today, and she wouldn't have to listen to another boring lecture. Miss Pergondie had arranged for the hour to be spent in the library. Jan liked libraries at any time, but she loved the Central High library during fifth hour for a special reason: Mike was the library aide.

Jan hadn't done any more work on her paper after she'd gotten back to the house the night before; she'd been too shaken up. Now she went up to the desk with a list of sources. She'd been able to get some of them from the public library, but she was still missing a few. "Any idea where I could find this stuff?" she asked, showing the list to Mike.

"Yeah, over here . . ." He led her to the history section, then glanced around. No one was in sight, so he leaned forward and gave her a quick kiss on the lips. "Best Class B in the state!" he whispered, grinning. She smiled back at him as he released her and consulted the list of titles. "You really want all this junk?" he asked. As he spoke, he reached up and pulled a book off the shelf. It was thick and looked old.

"Have to do the report, I guess." She took the book and glanced inside. "Not that it'll help my grade much. Pergondie has it in for me."

"She has it in for everyone," Mike corrected. The economics teacher was the least popular in the school. "But you have to pass economics to graduate."

"I don't think I will." Jan spoke without much interest. Knowing her mother and father wouldn't be there to see her get her diploma had killed most of the excitement of graduation.

Mike scowled at her. "Look, Jan, you have to graduate!"

"Why?" Jan asked in a reasonable voice.

He turned back to the shelf, straightening books unnecessarily. After a moment he spoke, his dark eyes still fixed on the books. "You have to pass so we can start college together. I thought we agreed on that."

Over a year earlier, they had decided they would go to Kenowa College, the local school, together. They'd filled out early admissions forms during their junior year; both had been accepted. Now Jan's acceptance was in jeopardy.

She replied obliquely, "I'm not sure I want to go to Kenowa now. I was thinking about trying for the University of Illinois." Her mother had been a history professor at the local college; Jan knew its campus almost as well as she knew Central High's. A different school might hold fewer painful memories. "We'd still get to see each other on weekends. It's only an hour's drive away."

"I know, but . . ." He got down the next book on Jan's list. "We'll have to work something out. Watch it, here comes Pergondie." By the time the economics teacher rounded the end of the bookshelves, Mike had handed several books to Jan and was consulting the list earnestly. He raised his voice slightly. "That's all we have here," he said, handing the list back to her. "You could try the city library."

Jan hadn't had a chance to tell Mike about the night before. Aware of the teacher's eyes on them, Jan mumbled thanks and went back to the desk. She'd tell him later. After checking out three of the books, she went to one of the tables and sat down with her notes.

For a while she tried to concentrate on the bone-dry text. But the words kept blurring on the page as her mind drifted. She overheard a couple of the other library aides, near the desk, talking about the Foote fire. There probably wasn't a kid in town who hadn't prowled through the extensive grounds there, trying to see into the boarded-up structure. One of the aides mentioned several small fires that had been set around town recently. Jan thought about the cardboard boxes she'd seen blazing when she woke up from sleepwalking.

Her eyes stared blankly at the page. Fire. She hated fire.

News of the *Cat Claws*'s award spread through the school quickly and replaced the fire as the main topic of conversation. The change was a welcome relief for Jan, since she didn't want to think about fire anymore.

Instead of getting over the first fire and her

parents' deaths, she was haunted by the past more and more. She couldn't talk to her new family about it. Aunt Leah would just make Jan drink more herb tea and quote bad poetry to her. All Aunt Leah really cared about anyway was Andrea. And Uncle Peter was almost never around; all *he* cared about was the business, Scott and Company. Andrea was her own age, but she and Jan had never been close enough to talk about *this* sort of thing.

By the end of the day, Jan was exhausted. That was almost normal, it had happened so often in the last month. She couldn't go home right away; there was the work session for the *Claws*. She went down to the journalism room as soon as the final bell rang. Soon she forgot her fatigue as the familiar business of layout and rewriting absorbed her. The entire staff, except for Barb, who had left school to take some pictures before the light faded, had stayed late. Mr. Buehler came in shortly after they started working, with some pizzas and soft drinks, turning the work session into another party. Well, they'd earned it. It wasn't every day that Kenowa Central won statewide prizes. Julie brought her tape player in, making it seem even more like a party. They used the biggest banner headline they'd ever printed to announce the award.

Once the paper was completed, the party went on for a little while, then everyone left for home. Jan and Mike were the last to leave. He had to take the paper to the printer and offered to drop her off on the way. Normally Jan would have gone with him, but not tonight. She had something to do on her way home. It was time to lay some ghosts to rest.

Barb Mitchell checked her light meter once again, then took another picture of what had been the parlor of the Foote mansion. The empty fireplace against a charred wall should make an interesting shot.

Barb jumped as a board creaked in the dining room—or what had once been the dining room. Someone else was poking around in the ruins. She wasn't doing any harm, but she didn't have permission to be there, which meant, technically, she was trespassing. Because the fire department had called the fire arson, she'd be in trouble if anyone caught her. Barb picked her way across the floor, testing her footing as she went, then relaxed as she caught sight of the other intruder. It was Jan

Scott. Barb was a bit surprised to see her there, since she'd have thought a burnt-out building would be the last place Jan would want to hang out. It hadn't been that long since her parents had died in a fire. But that was Jan's business. At least, Barb thought, Jan wasn't going to report her.

"Hey, Jan," Barb called. "Over here."

Jan ignored her, almost as though she hadn't heard. Barb framed Jan in the viewfinder as Jan stopped in front of a hole in the outside wall that had once been a long window. It would make a nice shot, with light from the setting sun angling in through the room. A tangle of bushes in the garden was visible through the gap in the wall, and Jan's dreamy expression made her look like something off the cover of a romance novel. Barb snapped the picture, wishing she could put Jan into a long white nightgown or something. The photo would be even more dramatic if she could. Then she called again.

"Jan! Wake up!"

It *was* strange, Jan wandering around here like that. . . .

Jan approached the house cautiously, but the cold smoke taste didn't trigger a nightmare. She hadn't been paying attention to where she was the previous night, and the smell had caught her unawares. This time she was ready.

During PE she'd had an idea. Recently one of the local TV stations had done a report on people who were afraid of flying. They were taught to conquer their fear by spending time in an airplane on the ground. After a month of training, they'd gone for a flight and hadn't panicked. The same sort of thing might help her. She wasn't ready to go near an actual fire, but poking around the destruction left by a fire might be like sitting on the ground in a parked airplane.

Near the house the rosebushes were shriveled from the blaze. Half-opened buds had turned into little black lumps along the green branches, and most of the thorns had burned. Jan stared at them. The roses weren't dead, but it would take time before new growth hid the damage. New growth. Staring at the blackened shrubbery, she found it hard to think of growth, or anything except the death that fire brought. This wasn't helping.

At least she was still awake. Jan followed the wall, cautiously avoiding fallen timbers and rubble. The old wood-frame building must have burned like a match. Her foot slipped on the edge of a wide hole, and she jumped across it awkwardly. Jan didn't want to fall into the basement. She might be trapped down there without a way out.

She stepped through what had once been the back door. The charred wood had been splintered by the fire fighters' axes. She pushed farther into the house, gingerly testing the steps up into the kitchen. They seemed solid enough to hold her. She passed into the old dining room. There were gaps and holes in the floor, and more in the outside walls. She knew she'd have to leave soon; the building could collapse at any minute.

Jan felt almost as though she were seeing double. In front of her was the devastation left by the fire, but layered over that, she could almost see the room the way it had been before. Even more faintly she could imagine the way things must have looked when the house was new. The combination of real and imagined was making her head hurt again, and Jan felt herself slipping into another waking nightmare. She could taste stale smoke, the same horrible acrid taste she'd been unable to get out of her throat for days after their fire. . . .

A voice behind Jan broke through the dream, startling her. She whirled around. "Barb! What are you doing here?"

"I'm wondering what *you're* doing here," Barb replied. "I called to you twice. Were you walking in your sleep or something?" She sounded concerned.

Jan flinched. She didn't want anyone to know about her nightly strolls. "I was just thinking about the last time I saw this place."

The distraction seemed to work. Barb glanced around at the smoke-blackened walls and the sagging ceiling panels. "You saw it before it was a mess? Wish I had."

"Once, a long time ago." Barb went back to her photography when it became obvious that Jan wasn't going to say anything else.

They left together, and Barb offered Jan a lift home. It was almost dark now. As they walked to the car, Barb said in a too-casual voice, "I was surprised to see you here. Well, I mean, I know how you must feel about fires. . . ." Her voice trailed off.

Jan got into the passenger seat. "It was the only old house left," Jan explained. "I wanted to see it, before they tore it down." Jan didn't want to talk about her family. Old buildings were a safer subject.

"It's sort of funny, when you think about it," Barb said. She started the car. "All those years, there were two really old houses in town, and now both of them are gone, almost at the same time. Like we couldn't have one if the other wasn't there."

"Yeah," Jan said, staring straight ahead.

"I wonder who started the fire," Barb said. "There've been a lot of them lately."

Jan didn't answer, but not because she hadn't heard. She wondered the same thing herself. What bothered Jan was the growing suspicion that all of the recent fires were tied together somehow. And tied to her, and to her sleepwalking.

31

THREE

The next day Mr. Kahn called Jan into his office during third hour. She'd always liked the guidance counselor; he was a good listener and treated kids like real people, not some sort of inferior species. But for several weeks she'd been avoiding him. She knew that her grades were a mess, but she couldn't make herself care. Mr. Kahn would care, though. It was his job.

When she got to his office, he had her records spread out in front of him on the desk. "Come on in, Jan," he greeted her. For once his familiar grin was missing.

She sat down across from him and started talking immediately. "Look, I know my grades are down, but it just doesn't matter that much anymore. Sorry to disappoint you."

"Disappoint me, Jan?" Mr. Kahn asked, leaning back in his chair. "Now that's something that really doesn't matter. I could say that what counts is not disappointing yourself, but if you don't care about it, that won't do much good, will it?" The chair squeaked as he suddenly shifted his weight, leaning forward. "How about disappointing your parents?"

"My parents are dead!" Jan said hotly, then stopped, stunned by her own outburst. She started to tremble.

"I know," he said quietly. "But you aren't. And I don't think they'd like to see you throwing your life away like this."

Jan's head fell forward, and she began to cry silently. He was right; she knew what her mother would have said about the way she'd given up.

When Mr. Kahn spoke again, it was in an easy, relaxed voice. "I think it might be time to reevaluate your plans. You might want to delay college for a semester or so. You could take some classes over, do a better job." He smiled at her. "Get some of your old fire back."

She flinched as though he'd struck her. "Oh,

damn," he swore under his breath. She raised her head. The look of horror on his face at what he'd said almost made her laugh. She managed a watery smile, and he muttered to himself some more. He was cussing himself out; she recognized the tone of voice even if she couldn't make out the words.

"I'm sorry," he said. "Occasionally I get my foot stuck in my mouth like that. I started to say, you've had enough stress in your life this year without worrying about four more years of school. You could start later. Meanwhile, take some classes here at Central and get yourself back together. I could write a letter to the college for you. I'm sure they'd understand."

It was a sensible suggestion. Jan opened her mouth to thank him and was appalled when instead she said, "I'm not getting myself together at all. I think I'm falling totally apart. The other day I walked home from the library, and I don't even remember it."

She hadn't intended to tell anyone about the frightening blank. Mr. Kahn was *too* easy to talk to. He looked thoughtful and said, "You wouldn't have mentioned it if you'd just been daydreaming or something. Obviously it upset you. Care to tell me how it happened, what you do remember?"

Everything poured out then: the bad dreams, the sleepwalking, the waking nightmare that had overtaken her on the way home from the library. Mr. Kahn listened quietly. When she finished, he sighed. "Jan, I'm a school counselor. I'm not a psychiatrist. But it doesn't take much training to see that all these fires lately are bothering you. Especially the one at the Footes'. It's not surprising; it takes time to get over something like losing your family. Have you talked to your doctor about any of this?"

"No!" She spoke quickly, then tried for a more reasonable tone. "I don't think I need to, not unless it gets worse. I'm not crazy or anything." She grinned at him, a forced grin he didn't return. "Like you said, I just need more time."

"There's nothing wrong with needing help, Jan," he said. "Anytime you want to talk, just come on in."

"Yeah." Jan stood up. She liked Mr. Kahn, but she regretted having said so much. She went back to class, leaving him staring at her records on his desk. She still hadn't decided anything about her future.

* * *

The only good thing about the day was that it was Friday. Mr. Kahn was right about what her parents would have said, but they weren't *here*, no matter how much she felt her mother's presence. And what if he called Aunt Leah? Jan didn't think he would; Mr. Kahn was pretty decent about keeping private stuff to himself. That was the last thing she needed, to have Aunt Leah thinking that she'd flipped out.

She turned in the rough draft of the economics report, knowing she'd done a superficial job. At least she wouldn't have a zero on the draft, and maybe she'd do better on the final paper.

All she wanted to do by the end of the day was go home, put on some music, and read for a while. But Julie Rodgers stopped her before she could leave the building. "Hey, Jan! I didn't see you after third hour. Don't forget, you and Andrea are invited tonight. See you at seven thirty, okay?" Spotting another friend down the hall, Julie yelled, "Hey, Christy! Wait up!" She ran toward the other girl before Jan could say anything.

Jan had forgotten all about the slumber party. She'd known the girls who would be there since grade school. Usually the parties were a lot of fun. With the way she'd been feeling lately, though, she wasn't in the mood. Besides, what if she walked in her sleep? She didn't need that sort of grief. Not that anyone slept much at a slumber party.

When Jan got home, Andrea was already packing her bag. "Do you think I should take an extra pillow?" she asked in lieu of a greeting. She shoved a couple of tapes into a side pocket and added, "Toss me my nightgown."

"Wouldn't hurt to take extra pillows," Jan answered. She got Andrea's gown from the bathroom and handed it to her. "Last time you wound up swiping mine, remember?"

She went into her own room, as Andrea called, "Well, if we both take an extra, that won't be a problem. Are you taking any tapes?"

"I don't think I'm going to go," Jan said.

In a moment her cousin was at the door. "How come?" she asked. "You didn't say anything earlier about not going."

"I'm not up for a party," Jan said. She was afraid Andrea wouldn't take that as an answer, and she was right.

"You get up for a party by going to a party," Andrea pointed out. "Are you sick or something?"

"I told you, I've been having headaches a lot," Jan answered. "Your mom's been bugging me about getting more sleep, and you know no one ever sleeps at a slumber party."

"Sure they do." Andrea grinned. "Just not very much. Besides, it's Friday night. We won't have to get up till noon tomorrow."

Jan still didn't feel like going, but she felt even less like having an argument. And explaining to Julie would be a hassle. A few hours later she and Andrea knocked at the Rodgerses' door. The party was already in progress. A carpet of sleeping bags and blankets covered the floor of the family room, the stereo was blasting, and the aroma of pizza flavored the air. Jan spotted several familiar flat boxes from the local carryout. Julie's parents were no place in sight. Jan figured they were upstairs in their bedroom, as far away from the noise as they could get without leaving. Julie's house was a favorite for slumber parties.

After a noisy debate over which movie to watch, they chose a comedy and settled down to watch and eat pizza. Andrea had been right, Jan decided; the way to get into a party mood was to go to a party. It was the type of silly movie that was more fun to watch in a group. As the characters on the screen thrashed around in a swimming pool full of suds, Jan wondered briefly why she'd even hesitated about coming. The movie ended with a long and complicated chase scene. Jan collapsed, giggling helplessly, and Julie had the hiccups from laughing so hard.

"Oh, owww," Barb moaned, holding her sides. "My ribs hurt."

"Did you see the prequel to this movie?" Sharon demanded. "It was better, I thought."

An argument broke out comparing the two films, punctuated with giggles as lines were quoted from each. A few girls helped themselves to more pizza, and some started getting ready for bed. Jan felt a slight dampening of her party mood as she went into the bathroom to change into her nightgown. The scars on her right arm and shoulder were still obvious and ugly, and she didn't want to let anyone see them. Fake scars were okay in movies, but no one wanted to see the real thing on someone they knew.

There were giggles, and a few girls hugged their pillows tightly as Barb turned out the lights and the next video started. Jan didn't like horror movies; after what she'd gone through, she couldn't enjoy phony fear. But she tried to match the mood of the group, shrieking when everyone else did and making comments about the gore. After all, horror films were as much a part of slumber parties as pizza.

Suddenly the scene shifted, and Jan closed her eyes as the madman villain thrust a burning torch into the face of his latest victim. The memory of the stench her arm had made as it burned filled Jan's nostrils. Pain flared as she stumbled toward the kitchen. She got there and leaned against the kitchen sink, head down, nearly losing the pizza she'd eaten earlier. She tried to control the clenching spasms of nausea. Her arm was throbbing.

"Jan?" Julie came in, hesitantly. Beyond, there was an abrupt silence in the family room. "Are you okay?"

Jan took a deep breath, trying to steady herself, then raised her head. Julie looked frightened, almost guilty. "Yeah, I'm all right. I just wasn't expecting that."

The guilt deepened on her friend's face. "None of us were. Look, I'm really sorry about it, Jan. We wouldn't try to, you know . . ."

Her voice trailed off, but Jan knew what she

meant. They wouldn't remind her of the fire and her family on purpose.

It didn't make Jan feel any better. It was no good, having people afraid to speak normally around her, like Mr. Kahn getting upset just for using the word "fire." Jan couldn't help it, though. Everything reminded her of the tragedy, and she reacted each time.

Still, there was no sense in ruining the night for everyone else. They'd turned off the VCR in the other room, and the whispers weren't the sort of normal goofing around that went on at a party. Sheri yelled, "Everything okay in there?"

Jan took a deep breath and cleared her throat. "Yeah, I'm fine," she called. "Don't worry about it; finish the tape." There was another moment's silence, then the sound track began again. Julie was still beside her, and Jan added, "Really, I'm all right. You go on. I'll just stay in here for a little while."

She reached for another can of cola. As she popped the tab, there was a faint tremor in her hands. Julie was watching closely and must have seen Jan's fingers trembling, but all she said was, "Are you sure? We don't have to watch the rest of this one, we've got plenty of other tapes. It's a stupid movie anyway."

"I'm sure," Jan said, nodding. "It's almost over, anyway. I'll just drink my Coke out here. Don't want to ruin the party." She was afraid she already had, or at least had thrown a shadow on it.

"Well . . . if you're positive . . ."

After a few more reassurances, Julie went back into the other room. There was a buzz of whispered conversation, almost drowning the sound effects of the movie. The volume had been lowered, and Jan couldn't tell what was happening in the show—and she didn't want to. Instead she stared out the window over the sink into the Rodgerses' dark backyard. She shouldn't have come.

A short while later, the lights came on in the family room and Jan rejoined her friends. Everyone was talking at the same time, about everything except the movie. Jan wondered if she should go home. But it was past midnight, and she was afraid that if she left, the rest of the party would be ruined, instead of salvaged, for the others. She tried to act as though nothing were wrong.

Her pretended party mood gradually shifted back to the real thing. Andrea and Sharon dished out ice cream for everyone, and more cans of soda were passed around. By common consent horror movies were ignored. Instead Barb chose another movie that most of the girls had seen several times before, but which they were all ready to see again. The sound track on this one was by Julie's favorite band, and she cranked the volume so high, her mother came in to complain. Over Julie's protests the sound was lowered again.

By the end of the film, the party was back to normal. It was almost three o'clock, and yawns were beginning to outnumber laughs. With some shoving and tickling, the group settled down and the lights were turned out. Barb and Sharon kept talking in whispers for a while, but Jan was more than ready for sleep. The day had been too long.

When she closed her eyes, Jan saw the horrible images from the movie again. Special effects blurred with the memory of her arm, flames wrapped around it like a blanket. Her eyes snapped open. No sleep at all would be better than these instant replays.

The other girls were quiet now, as gentle snores surrounded her. Jan stared up at the beamed ceiling, her eyes wide open as she fought the pictures in her mind.

Her thoughts were bitter. There wasn't an end to it, never any end. She couldn't even go to a party without something happening to spoil it for her. Happiness was beginning to seem like a myth, something she had made up when she was a little kid, like an imaginary playmate. Eventually, her eyes closed, and she drifted off to sleep.

A coughing fit woke Jan up as she inhaled smoke. For a moment confused scraps of dreams fogged her mind. She'd had another nightmare, reliving the fire again, seeing herself burning. She took a step forward. Another eddy of smoke closed around her, and she coughed again, her mouth dry from the searing heat and the smoke. Finally she woke up enough to realize it wasn't a bad dream. The nightmare was in front of her, as flames shot from the roof of the building a few feet away.

Jan blinked against the sting of the smoke. Where was she? The smoke thinned for a moment as she backed away, and she recognized the building. How did she get here? She was a block or so from Julie's, in front of a restaurant that had been closed for a few months. As she watched, the front plate-glass window shattered, shards flying past her. She gasped as one grazed her right arm. A thin line of blood followed the rip in her sleeve. As her left hand closed over the wound, she realized she was in her nightgown. And her feet were bare.

"Jan! Are you hurt?" Julie's voice startled her. "C'mon, let's get *out* of here." She grabbed Jan and pulled her roughly down the sidewalk. When they were a safe distance away, she stopped and looked Jan over.

"You're bleeding," Julie told her. Jan just stared at her. "Did you get hit by the glass?"

"I'm . . . I don't . . . ," Jan stammered.

Julie took her limp hand. "Let me see . . . no, it doesn't look too bad." She dropped Jan's hand and briefly looked into her eyes. "Are you awake now?"

"I think so," Jan said. Even from a distance she could feel the heat of the fire through the thin fabric. She saw Andrea standing on the other side of Julie.

"We'd better get out of here. I can hear sirens." Julie tugged at Jan's good hand. "I don't want to be caught hanging around. With all the arson lately, the cops are going to really come down on anyone they catch near a fire." She looked past Jan at Andrea, with an expression Jan couldn't read. But she was afraid she knew what Julie was thinking.

Jan could hear the siren, now that she was awake enough to sort dream from reality. They headed for the Rodgerses' house, starting to run as the sirens drew nearer. The bizarre sight of three girls running down the street in their nightgowns at this hour would certainly earn some questions from the fire fighters converging on the Blue Willow Restaurant.

The three girls reached Julie's house and stopped in the yard, looking back down the block toward the fire. The first truck arrived, luckily coming from the other direction.

Jan was afraid to ask Julie, but she had to know. "How . . . do you know how I got there? I don't remember anything after I went to sleep."

Andrea answered for Julie, her voice low and expressionless. "You were walking in your sleep again, Jan."

"Again?" Julie blurted out. "Jan, have you walked in your sleep before? What's it like?"

"Sometimes," Jan said, just as Andrea said, "She always has." They both stopped, then Jan continued speaking. Since Andrea had already given it away, Jan answered candidly, "I've always done it when I was upset, ever since I was a little kid." She looked at Andrea, who stood motionless. "I'm not really sure how much. Sometimes I get back to bed without waking up, and then I don't really know I've done it at all. I don't know what it's *like;* I'm asleep when it happens."

"You've done a lot of it lately," Andrea said quietly. "I've watched you, and I've seen you come in and go right up the stairs, sound asleep. I got worried tonight. You'd been gone over half an hour."

"Half an hour?" It was worse than she thought.

"At least. I woke Julie up and told her I was worried, and we came out looking for you."

"You were just standing there, Jan, just standing there sound asleep." Julie sounded concerned, but there was an undercurrent of fascinated, horrified delight. Jan wanted to shout "Boo!" and see if Julie would jump. Julie was looking at her as if she were one of the monsters in the movie they'd watched that evening.

A second fire truck arrived as a couple of the

47

other girls came out onto the front porch. Some of Julie's neighbors were out in their yards as well, and lights came on up and down the block as sirens continued to pierce the night air.

"Hey . . . what's going on . . . there's a fire! Oh, wow . . . I'm going back to bed, I'm *tired* . . . what's burning . . ." There was a babble of voices as the rest of the slumber party tumbled off the porch, surrounding the three in the front yard. Safety in numbers, Jan thought. They wouldn't spot the girl who'd walked right up to the fire in her sleep when she was hidden by so many other girls in nightclothes.

Under cover of the noise, Jan tugged on Julie's robe. "Julie, please don't tell anyone else I was sleepwalking, will you? Please?"

Julie didn't answer. Down the street fire fighters in bright slickers were dragging hoses from the trucks to the fire hydrants. Her eyes still on the fire, she asked, "Why not?"

"People wouldn't understand," Jan said. She felt as though she were pleading. "Sleepwalking's perfectly normal."

"Yeah, right, everyone does it all the time," Julie said sarcastically. "What do you mean, normal? Jan, I don't understand. Do you have some sort of mental problem?" Behind the

48

words Jan heard the real question, *Are you crazy?*

"No, I'm not crazy if that's what you're thinking. It just happens. That's all, I walk in my sleep." Jan paused for a moment, then repeated, "Please, Julie. Don't tell the others."

After what felt like hours, Julie nodded slowly. "All right, Jan, I guess I won't say anything now. But I think you should see a doctor." Her tone said, *a head doctor.*

"Thanks," Jan said. Julie shook her head and went over to some of the other girls. Most of the neighborhood was outside now, watching the fire.

"Hey, Barb," someone yelled, "are you going to take any pictures for the *Claws?*"

"I don't have my camera!" Barb snarled.

There was a general laugh at this. Barb and Julie were both on the paper with Jan, and Sheri suggested one of them write it up for the paper. Under cover of all the talk, Andrea slipped in next to Jan. She leaned close and said, "Maybe you were right about not coming. Do you think you're going to do anything else tonight? In your sleep, I mean?"

Jan shrugged. "How do I know?"

It was as Jan had told Julie; she didn't know

49

what was happening when she was asleep. And that fact was beginning to scare her. If she could get up and out of a room full of sleeping girls, and not even know she was doing it, could she be doing anything else?

Before long the fire was extinguished, and the excitement died down. People started drifting back into their houses, and the slumber party went back to the Rodgerses' family room. Julie stopped Jan for a moment on the front porch.

"Jan, I said I won't tell anyone, and I won't. But I was just wondering." Julie paused, her eyes on the scene down the street, where the fire fighters were rewinding the hose. "Do you ever do anything besides walking when you're asleep?"

"I don't know," Jan whispered. The unspoken question hung on the air. *Did Jan start fires in her sleep?*

FOUR

Even though the sun was almost rising, everyone went back to bed. Back to bed, perhaps, but not back to sleep. Jan didn't dare. *Let's face it,* she thought, *I'm not afraid of sleepwalking. I'm afraid of what else I might do.* She couldn't remember setting the fire. She didn't really believe she had. But the fear persisted.

Jan didn't know much about sleepwalking, even though she'd done it occasionally for most of her life. Her parents had never worried about it; in fact, it had almost been a family joke. Her father had also been a sleepwalker as a child. Since it usually happened when Jan was upset, her folks used it as a barometer of her emotions. They would try to find out why she was upset, but they didn't worry about the sleepwalking itself.

Their relaxed attitude had vanished with them. Jan had moved in with her relatives after a few days in the hospital. The night after the funeral, Jan had walked, and Aunt Leah had been horrified. She read all the pop-psychology books that came out and was convinced the sleepwalking meant that Jan had deep mental problems. She asked so many questions about the way Jan felt and what she dreamed about that Jan thought she really *would* go crazy. Her family doctor had given Jan some medicine, and after that the sleepwalking stopped. Aunt Leah had taken the credit, claiming she'd solved the problems by following the suggestions in the books. Jan didn't argue. She hadn't told her aunt about the trip to the doctor's office.

The mysterious fires lately had started around the same time that Jan had begun to sleepwalk again. She felt the same way she did when she had a cold and had to take deconges- tants—fuzzy all the time. Was it possible that she really had been setting fires in her sleep? She hated fire, but she'd been there watching the restaurant burn, and twice she'd gone by the Foote ruins. Maybe she was attracted by what she hated, the same way birds were supposed to be fascinated by snakes.

Despite her intention of staying awake, Jan fell asleep, but not before the room had filled with the light of a gray dawn. When she woke up, most of the girls were awake and rolling up their sleeping bags and blankets. A few were still asleep; in the corner only the very top of Andrea's head was visible above the edge of her blanket. Jan yawned. Smoke lingered on her nightgown. She hated that smell. She hurried to change into her other clothes. Maybe the rip could be mended and the smoke washed out of the nightgown, but the bloodstain on the sleeve was there for good. Scratch one nightgown.

Jan went into the kitchen, where Julie was helping her mom make pancakes. Jan accepted a plate, although she was almost too tired to be hungry. She squinted at the clock on the stove. Eleven o'clock. Between nightmares and sleepwalking and the excitement of the fire, she doubted if she'd slept four hours.

Jan lost what little appetite she had when the hourly news update came on the radio with news about the Blue Willow fire. Inevitably, it had been another case of arson. The report referred to the recent incidents as a "series" of fires, and unnamed sources said all of them were probably linked. Speculation broke out among the girls around the table. Jan's fears came back, full strength. She poked again at her half-eaten pancake, then shoved the plate back. Raising her eyes, she saw Julie watching her. The last bite stuck in Jan's throat. Julie was staring at her with questions in her eyes, questions that Jan was afraid to answer.

In the afternoon, girls started leaving in twos and threes. Julie hadn't said anything more to Jan about finding her in front of the burning restaurant the night before, and no one else had mentioned anything about sleepwalking. Julie must have kept her promise not to tell. Still, Jan was uneasy. It was just a matter of time before everyone found out.

Her arm was sore where the flying glass had sliced it. The cut was right across the worst scars from the earlier fire. Several times that day, Jan touched it gingerly. She knew it was just a coincidence, but the new injury on top of the old scars held significance for her. Twice now fire had left its mark on her. She just hoped the marks didn't go deeper.

Andrea was surly and bad-tempered for most

of the afternoon; she hadn't slept much either. Jan's headache came back, a throbbing at the top of her skull that matched her pulse. Aunt Leah drove Jan frantic by insisting she drink another herbal concoction. Jan choked a part of the bitter stuff down, then poured the rest out when her aunt wasn't looking. As nasty as it was, it did help; Jan's headache subsided, leaving her sleepy. She went to bed early in the evening, so exhausted she didn't care if she marched down Main Street in her sleep. As long as she could get some rest.

She slept, but she still felt tired on Sunday. The sour taste in her mouth was matched by the sour feeling that she'd had another bad dream. Jan couldn't remember anything about it, but for several hours after she got up, everything seemed slightly out of focus and unreal. Nightmares usually left her feeling that way. Her head felt as though it were filled with cobwebs.

After lunch Mike came over. He suggested some fresh air to wake her up, and they decided to go for a drive. It wasn't a pleasant day; the seasons seemed to have reversed themselves, with spring giving way to winter. The sky was gray with clouds that promised a late snow.

Even so, Mike was right. Getting out did make her feel a little better. Once they were out of town, Mike pushed the accelerator almost to the floor, and they sped down the back roads, level fields stretching to the horizon. Kenowa was in the heart of the Illinois farm belt. Soon the city would be surrounded by fields of corn so tall it blocked the horizon.

They drove through one of the countless small towns that dotted the area and stopped at a small state park. It was one of their favorite spots, woods surrounding a small man-made lake. There were only a few hardy fishermen out in rowboats, braving the chill, and Jan and Mike had the picnic area to themselves. The buds on the trees were almost ready to open, despite the cold temperature. Jan took a deep breath of the clammy air and turned to Mike.

"Thanks," she said. "You were right. I needed to get out."

He sat down at the base of a tree and pulled her down beside him. "I'm also right about us going to Kenowa College together." Ever since that day in the library, he kept bringing the subject up. "And you know it."

"No, I don't know it," she said. "If I do go to college, I'm going someplace else. I'm not going to put up with even more reminders, Mike. Kenowa was Mom's school. Not mine."

His face had that stubborn look again, the one he got when he was convinced he was right. "Jan, I loved them too. You know I got along better with your parents than I do with my mom and Arnie, but you can't run from everything that reminds you of them. It won't work."

She shook her head without speaking. She knew this wasn't running away. Going to Kenowa College this soon after her parents' death would be like picking a scab. The wound needed time to heal. Jan leaned back against his shoulder, not wanting to talk about it anymore. As much as she loved Mike, he had his faults. One was that he wanted everything to be the way it had been when they'd first made their plans together. Things *weren't* the same, and they never would be.

Mike was persistent. He brought the subject up several more times, until Jan snapped that since she wasn't likely to graduate, worrying about college didn't make much sense. By the time they went back, Jan was seething. They'd had a few fights in the past, but those had been more explosive, fast to start and as fast to finish.

This felt serious. And she was sure she was right. Maybe someday she'd be able to face the school where her mother had taught, but not yet. Not yet.

That night Jan woke up standing at the top of the stairs in front of Andrea's open door. She whimpered without realizing she'd made a sound. It had happened again. She reached the door of her own room just as Andrea came out into the hall.

"Are you awake?" Andrea asked tiredly. "Good, go back to bed and let the rest of us get some sleep."

Jan bit her lips. "I'm sorry, did I wake you up?"

"No, I'm talking in my sleep." The sarcasm stung. "Of course you woke me up! First when you bumped my door on your way out, then just now when you came back. I don't care if you want to go jogging in your sleep, I just wish you'd do it quietly."

Jan repeated herself. "Sorry." A new thought struck her. "Did you follow me?"

"Why should I? All I want to do is get a full night's sleep, without you banging in and out!"

Andrea went back into her own room and slammed the door.

Jan lay down and pulled the blankets up. She wished Andrea had followed her. It might be the only way Jan would ever find out what she was doing.

The next afternoon Jan ditched school and went to see Dr. Holsinger. The doctor had treated Jan as far back as she could remember, although she didn't see her very often these days, since Aunt Leah didn't believe in M.D.'s. Jan didn't have an appointment, but she hoped they could squeeze her in. She sat in the waiting room for almost two hours, leafing through various magazines. Finally the nurse said, "Janelle? Dr. Holsinger will see you now."

They went through the ritual of weight and temperature, then Jan sat on the end of the examining table to wait some more. The doctor strode into the room after about fifteen minutes. "Hello, Jan," she said. Dr. Holsinger had a lot of patients, and she was always in a hurry, but she still made time to chat. "We haven't seen you in here in a while. What's the problem?"

"Can I get some more of that medicine?" Jan wanted to avoid a long explanation. "The stuff to keep me from walking in my sleep?"

"Clonazepam. What's the matter, are you do-ing it again?" The doctor pushed her short steel-gray hair back and looked at Jan curiously. "When did this start?"

Jan shrugged, embarrassed. "I'm not sure. A couple weeks ago, maybe. I can't find the pre-scription bottle from the last time. I think I used it all."

Dr. Holsinger's lips pursed for a moment. "That's pretty potent stuff, Jan. I really hate to prescribe it if it's not needed. Suppose you tell me a little more. How sure are you that you've been sleepwalking?" Bit by bit she extracted the details from Jan. The one thing Jan held back was the frightening blackout she'd had on the way home from the library. That and her growing suspicion that she herself was the ar-sonist.

Finally the doctor said, "Well, I'll give you a prescription and we'll see how it works. But don't take more than one tablet at a time, even if you do keep sleepwalking, and call me if you have any trouble. This drug's a depressant; among other things it's likely to make you sleepy. Don't try driving after you take it." She scribbled a prescription and handed it to Jan, then said, "One more thing. I suspect all these

60

fires have you upset. That's probably what got you started again. But if it goes on too much longer, you might want to think about seeing a psychologist."

Jan shook her head. She was almost afraid to dig too deeply into her subconscious under the circumstances. Besides, she was still a minor. Her relatives would probably have to sign something before a psychologist could see her. Aunt Leah wouldn't, and Uncle Peter always followed her lead.

Jan made an appointment to come back in a couple of weeks, then got the prescription filled on the way home. That night she took the first dose with a feeling of relief. Maybe now she could get a full night's sleep.

The medicine worked. At least Jan didn't wake up out of bed anytime during the next few days. She felt a little drowsy, but she expected that, and it was better than wondering what she was doing at night. The first indication Jan had that the medicine might not be doing the job came a few mornings after she'd started taking it. She woke up and put her feet into her slippers, then pulled them back out quickly. The slippers were clammy. Jan picked them up and examined them. There was damp mud on the soles, and a line of faint muddy footprints led across the floor, from the door to her bed. As far as Jan could tell, she'd slept dreamlessly all night. But her slippers couldn't have gone for a stroll by themselves.

Mike came by that night. When he walked in, he took one horrified look at her in her sloppy, comfortable sweats and exclaimed, "Jan, come on! The show starts at eight thirty, and it'll take at least an hour to get there!"

"What show?" As his expression changed to anger, she said, "Oh, yeah," and ran for the stairs. She burst into Andrea's room and asked, "Mike's here, he said something about a show. Do you know what he's talking about?"

Andrea looked up from the video she was watching and said, "The White Lion concert in Springfield. He got tickets. Don't you remember? I told you about it last night."

Jan didn't remember. She ran into her room, stripping off her sweats as she went and fighting the nausea that gripped her. She had wanted to go to the concert, but it had been sold out for weeks. Mike must have found a couple of people who couldn't use their tickets. She dressed quickly, shoving her head under the faucet to rinse the short curls. Thank heavens she didn't have to do much with her hair; there wasn't time. But her stomach continued to knot. She was sure she wouldn't have forgotten something like this, but there was a complete blank in her memory. She went back through Andrea's room and asked, "You told me? When?"

Her cousin hit the pause button and stared at her, mouth hanging open. "Jan, he called last night, and I thought you were already asleep, so I took the message. Then I came up here and you were working on your computer, so I went in and told you about it. You didn't seem very interested, and I said I'd go with him if you didn't want to, and you told me Mike was your boyfriend, as if I didn't know that. We must have talked for five minutes. Are you telling me you don't *remember*?"

Numbly Jan shook her head. She couldn't remember any of it. Then Mike called from downstairs, "Jan, come on!" She decided she'd worry about it later. She took the stairs two at a time. Mike was already in the car, and he took off with a squeal of tires as he tried to make up for lost time.

On the way to the concert, Jan told him about her memory lapse. She didn't want to, but there was no other way of explaining her failure to remember the date, unless she lied and said Andrea hadn't told her.

He was silent for several miles after she finished. Then he said, "But how could you have forgotten about it?"

Jan blinked against the tears threatening to ruin her eye makeup. She knew how ridiculous it sounded. "I told you, I think it was that medicine, the stuff to keep me from sleepwalking."

"I thought you said it just made you sleepy," Mike said.

"Well, maybe I forgot because I was asleep!" Jan snapped. "Look, I'm sorry it happened. But it's over and we're going to the show, so let's just forget about it." The word "forget" rang hollowly in Jan's ears.

After a few more miles, Mike spoke again. He sounded reluctant, as though he didn't like what he was saying, but he went ahead anyway. "You can forget it, maybe—you've been forgetting a lot of things. But I don't think I can. Jan, I think you need to see a doctor. Not Dr. Holsinger. A . . ." He searched for a word. "A specialist."

"No!" It came out too loud. Jan dropped her voice and continued, "You mean a shrink, don't you? A psychiatrist. I don't need one, I just have to watch it with that medicine."

They drove the rest of the way in silence. Despite what she'd said, Jan was afraid Mike was right. The concert was loud enough to keep her awake; in fact, the volume brought on another headache. She'd been looking forward to seeing the band in concert for a long time, but her mood threw a damper on the entire evening. She fell asleep in the car coming home.

Jan's slippers were damp again later in the week, and the hem of her robe was muddy as well. She thought about calling Dr. Holsinger, but decided not to. Side effects from the medicine were one thing, but this was a little more serious than just forgetting a few things and doing some nighttime wandering. As incidents continued—conversations with Andrea she couldn't recall, windows open that she'd left closed, things left out that she remembered putting away—Jan seriously considered the possibility that she was losing her mind.

Don't they say that if you think you're going crazy, you aren't?, she wondered. Jan was sure she'd read that someplace, but that didn't mean it was true.

Mental illness was just a disease, she knew that, but it was a scary thing, not being in control of her own actions. There were deeper fears, but Jan wasn't ready to face them.

She focused on what had happened the night of the slumber party. One practical argument against her guilt was that Jan wasn't sure she'd know how to burn down a building when she was awake. Even if she was crazy, how could she have started a fire in her sleep? Jan rummaged through the newspaper and found the report on the fire. The arson investigator said an "accelerant" had been used on the blaze. Further on he used the term again, then explained that in this case, it looked as though it had been gasoline.

You could get gasoline everywhere. And you didn't need to be a professional arsonist to use it. A few rags and some gasoline and *poof.* Instant fire. Even Jan knew how to siphon it out of a gas tank. Her dad had taught her the trick once when the lawn mower had run out of gas. But she didn't think she could have done that and stayed asleep. Even sleepwalking had its limits; the smell and taste of gasoline would have awakened her. She put the newspaper away with a sigh of relief.

She sat down to work on a poem she'd started the week before. Jan enjoyed writing articles for the *Cat Claws*. Occasionally she tried fiction, which was a lot of fun. But above all she loved writing poetry. She always felt as though the real Janelle Scott came out then.

She started her word processor, saving a backup copy of the old version automatically. Older versions came in handy if she decided she didn't like her changes. The opening lines of her poem appeared on the screen.

A purple flavor, iris blossoms
Color the air delicately.
Soon daffodils will test their yellow
Against the springtime sun . . .

The flowers wouldn't bloom for several weeks yet, but she wanted to have the poem ready before then. The last part of it still didn't feel right. She moved down the screen, scrolling the lines, then stopped, her hands frozen on the keyboard. These weren't her words. . . .

Purple the color of bruises,
it's ugly ugly ugliness

67

and then when it blooms it rots
and it's dead like a dead fire
that's eating the flowers
and the people and the world
and the ugly fire is better than flowers . . .

She broke free of her paralysis and quickly scrolled down. The words became less coherent, losing even the pattern of a poem and drifting into obscenities Jan never even thought. The additions were grafted onto her original poem, like an extra stanza, but turned the poem into something hideous. She'd tried in her poem to sound more hopeful and optimistic than she'd felt since her parents' deaths. This addition was out of her worst nightmares.

Jan deleted all the lines that came after her original ending, then saved the file. Her computer automatically added a date and time to each file she saved, and she looked at the original file once more. She hadn't worked on it in over a week. But the last time stamp on the file was from the night before the concert. Jan looked at it and felt a chill.

The last time the poem had been worked on was around the same time Andrea had told her about the concert. Jan didn't remember the conversation, and she couldn't remember working on the poem. She was sure she hadn't written anything like this. But the time stamp contradicted her mutely. Whether she could remember it or not, these words had been added to her poem that night.

FIVE

Finding the distorted poem upset Jan even more than the bad dreams and sleepwalking had. In the movies this would all turn out to be the work of some monster or demon. Jan wished she could believe she'd fallen into one of those movies. Even the worst ones were less scary than what she was afraid of: that she herself was the monster.

Rumors about the fires and Jan had started to float around the school. Jan wasn't sure if Julie had broken her promise, or if Andrea had said something, but her friends seemed embarrassed to be around her these days. Barb asked her point-blank if there was any truth to the rumors that she'd been around the Blue Willow the night of the slumber party. Jan had lied and said no. She didn't want to tell the whole world about her problems. Barb hadn't seemed very convinced, and Jan realized she'd wasted a lie. It was stupid anyway; denials never stopped rumors. Besides, if she was capable of writing and carrying on conversations without being able to remember it . . .

If she was capable of that, then anything was possible. She'd been trying to hide her deepest fear from herself, but now it pushed its way to the surface. The authorities had never determined the cause of the fire that had killed her parents. If she was guilty of setting the recent fires, she could have set that one as well. Had she killed her own parents?

"Morning, Aunt Leah," Jan said, sitting down at the breakfast table. She held out her cup for her aunt to fill. The morning herb tea was one of the few palatable ones Aunt Leah fixed, and even if it didn't have the kick of coffee, it might help wake her up. The last few days, Jan had been dragging again, as tired as she'd been a few weeks earlier when she'd been wandering every night.

"Jan, you look dreadful," said Aunt Leah, pouring tea. "No arguments this time; you're

71

going to start taking blood builder." She left the table and returned with a large gelatin capsule. "Take it." She held it out to Jan, who was too tired to put up a fight about it. She swallowed the bulky pill with a scalding sip of her tea.

Uncle Peter and Andrea arrived in the dining room together. As Uncle Peter took his seat, he said, "Jan, you've been sleepwalking again, haven't you?"

Jan's heart sank. She just sat there, trying to think of an answer. Finally she said, "I was a few weeks ago, but I don't remember doing it lately. I got some more medicine from Dr. Holsinger."

"You went to the doctor's without having the courtesy to even mention it to me?" Aunt Leah asked sharply. "Jan, we're responsible for you now. I expect you to tell *me* when you're sick, instead of going to a stranger."

I know Dr. Holsinger better than I know you, Jan thought. And anyway, her aunt was impossible to talk to about even simple things. How was Jan supposed to have brought up her sleepwalking? *"I think I've gone crazy, please pass the butter."*

"I'm sorry," she said. "Uncle Peter, did Dr.

72

Holsinger call you?" Jan had to know how he'd found out.

"You left the back door open last night," he said. "Rain was blowing in when I woke up."

Jan looked over and saw what she'd missed before, damp spots where water had been mopped up and her soaked slippers, right beside the door. It was no wonder Uncle Peter knew who'd left it open.

Aunt Leah and Uncle Peter took turns lecturing Jan throughout breakfast. School was no better. Mr. Buehler asked her twice for her homework before she heard him. When she did, she couldn't find the paper. During math she overheard Christy and Sharon whispering about her while they were working in study teams. They'd both been at the slumber party, and it was obvious from the whispers and glances they shot her way that they knew what had happened during the night there. Miss Pergondie gave them a test in economics. Jan hadn't studied for it at all and spent most of the hour staring at the page, unable even to make sense of the questions. The paper she handed in was almost blank.

By the end of the week, Jan wanted to run away from everyone. She hadn't found herself wandering at night, but from the evidence—wet slippers, her bookcase emptied onto the floor, doors open—it happened several more times. Andrea referred casually to a conversation Jan couldn't recall having. Her cousin had denied telling anyone about Jan's sleepwalking, which meant Julie must have broken her promise. Jan couldn't ask her about it; Julie had been avoiding her since the party. And Mike . . .

On Thursday she'd had her worst fight ever with Mike. He'd tried to get her to go see another doctor, one that specialized in emotional problems. "He's supposed to be really good," Mike had said when he'd handed Jan the phone number. "Maybe he can help with the nightmares and—stuff."

Jan had promised Aunt Leah she wouldn't go to another doctor without arranging it through her, and she didn't intend to break the promise. But when she'd tried to explain this to Mike, he had refused to accept it.

"Look, I don't care if they are your legal guardians, you can at least talk to him. Or if you don't want to see him, at least talk to Mr. Kahn again. I got this guy's name from his office anyway. He could probably help some."

"You're saying I'm crazy." Her own bitterness had surprised Jan, since she actually believed the same thing.

"I didn't say you were crazy," Mike insisted. "I just said you needed help."

Mike's tone of voice, his careful gentleness, had contradicted the words. She knew there was something seriously wrong when he treated her as though she were emotional spun glass. The quarrel ended with Jan yelling at Mike that she wasn't crazy and that even if she was, it was none of his business.

He hadn't spoken to her since.

Mike finally broke the silence on Sunday afternoon. He came over unannounced, but Jan was still happy to see him. They both started to apologize at once, then stopped, embarrassed.

There were silent reminders of the fight in what they didn't talk about, and Jan was afraid it wasn't over yet. How could it be, when she was still waking up every morning with nightmare hangovers, wondering where she'd been during her sleep?

A little while after Mike had arrived, Jan asked him if he'd heard any gossip about her at school.

"We've been going together a long time,

Jan," Mike started. "Nobody's going to bad-mouth you to me."

"I can think of a few who would," Jan argued.

His neck turned brick-red. "Oh, sure, there're a few idiots who never keep their mouths shut, but I don't listen to that crap, Jan, you know that."

"I wasn't asking you to defend me. I just want to know what people are *saying*."

"Nothing that makes any sense . . ."

"Mike," she interrupted him firmly. "Tell me."

"All right," he finally said. "I don't know how, but everyone in school knows you walk in your sleep, and the ones with no brains seem to think you're crazy or something."

"You mean I'm not?" Jan's mouth twisted wryly. "You could have fooled me. . . . Go on."

"That's it, more or less." He took a deep breath. "Just that you flipped out after, well, after the fire. . . ."

That was all he could, or would, tell her. He didn't mention any names, but it didn't really matter who had started the rumors. The story was out.

Mike needed to type up an article he was

working on, so they went up to Jan's room to use her computer. While he typed the story, Jan worked on her math assignment for the next day. As she struggled with the problems, she thought about Mike's suggestion. Seeing a doctor was probably a good idea. Jan wouldn't call the psychologist—her agreement with Aunt Leah still ruled that out—but she'd go in and see Mr. Kahn this week. Maybe she'd try delayed admission. The math problem she was working on fell neatly into place, and she went on to the next one.

"Jan," Mike called from the computer, "come tell me what this is about." His voice was strained.

She got up and went over beside him. He'd printed out his article for the *Chronicle* and had another file on the screen. Jan looked at the title. It was a short story she'd been messing around with for months. She glanced down the screen and stiffened with shock. She didn't recognize any of those sentences, but they reminded her of the poem.

There was violence and obscenity. And fire. Everything ended in fire.

She raised horror-filled eyes to Mike. He was

watching her, his face grim. "Jan, what's this about?"

She shook her head. She knew it was hopeless, but there wasn't anything she could do except tell the truth. "I've never seen it before."

"Don't give me that. Your file, your computer, your room, your story . . . Jan, this stuff is *sick*!"

"Mike, I don't recognize any of this," Jan protested. Her eyes drifted back to the screen. That was the right word, all right. Sick. "I haven't even looked at this story in weeks."

He pulled up the directory that listed every file and program on the computer. Silently he pointed to the listing for the story. The last time the file had been changed was two days before, at three seventeen A.M. As far as Jan knew, she'd been in bed, sound asleep, at that time. Was Dr. Holsinger's medicine really keeping her from sleepwalking, or was it just keeping her from remembering it?

Jan woke up that night, heart pounding and imaginary sirens ringing in her ears. She sat up and swung her feet over the edge of the bed. Her slippers weren't there. When she turned on the light, she saw them by the bathroom door. She went over and picked them up, then shuddered as she slipped a hand into one. It was still warm inside; it had just been taken off a foot.

Jan shivered as a cool breeze raised goose bumps on her arm. Stepping out into the hall to see where the draft was coming from, she peered down the stairs. Light from the street-lamp on the corner was shining in through the open front door, broken by the moving shadow of branches. Jan crept down the stairs, not sure if this was reality or another dream, and closed the door.

Back in her room, she caught a faint but un-mistakable smell of gasoline. Jan sniffed, casting around for the scent like a dog. She followed the scent to her robe, tossed on the floor at the foot of her bed. The left sleeve was damp.

Jan didn't go back to bed. She spent the rest of the night reading with all the lights on. When morning came, she was too tired to go to school. Pleading sickness, she crawled back into bed. Andrea came in to get Jan's assignments, promising to turn them in. When she left for school, she forgot to turn off her radio. Jan listened without much interest, trying to relax after the night's tensions, until the newscast came on.

Fire investigators had found a pile of gas-soaked rags in a cardboard box, next to the library. They were calling it attempted arson.

The next day Jan had a doctor's appointment, but this one had the grudging approval of her aunt. She was still undergoing treatment from a plastic surgeon for the burn scars on her arm. The doctor was a specialist at reducing the disfiguration left by severe burns. While Jan's arm was completely functional, she hadn't worn a short-sleeved or sleeveless blouse since the fire.

At midmorning she checked into the hospital for outpatient surgery. After waiting for what seemed like hours, the doctor arrived and surgery began. The anesthetics affected her more strongly this time than they usually did. The local, which should only have numbed her arm, made her sleepy instead. Probably, Jan decided, it was because of all the sleep she'd missed recently. Her arm would hurt horribly for a few days, but maybe the pain medicine would let her catch up on rest.

She was still sleepy when she went home, fresh bandages swathing her arm. Aunt Leah fussed over her, but for once she didn't try to

force any of her herb teas down Jan's throat. Jan
went straight to bed.

*Her arm was hurting, burning. She saw
flames licking at it. Every place they touched her
skin, they left a red mark that flared as brightly
as the flames. In the distance she could hear the
sirens. The fire danced around the walls of her
room, reaching around the closed door to the
hallway and the silent smoke detector.*

*As she sat up, the pain suddenly subsided.
The room was smaller, free of the orange glow
of the fire. A cool blue light washed over her
from the computer monitor on the desk. Blue,
like the blue of the sea. The seawater must have
put out the fire.*

*"Water." She heard her own voice croaking
the word and almost laughed. She sounded so
hoarse, so sleepy. The other girl handed her the
glass. It was so silly to be drinking water from a
glass, with the blue light flowing through the
room like the sea. Why didn't she just open her
mouth? She tried, and water slopped into it from
the glass.*

*The room assumed a more solid shape around
her. It wasn't her old room, and it wasn't on fire.*

Water wasn't flooding through it, just the light from her monitor. It shouldn't be on in the middle of the night, but she felt too sleepy to go shut it off. "Andrea, shut off the computer."

"Shhhh. I will, don't worry." The other girl approached her. "Do you need more medicine?"

Medicine. Medicine to stop the pain, to stop the dreams, to stop the fire. Her arm hurt. She took the pill and swallowed it. She handed the glass back. "More water." She drank the water, but her mouth still felt dry.

"Lie down, Jan," the other girl whispered. "Go back to sleep." Obedient, sleepy, Jan lay back against the pillow. She imagined her short red curls looked like flames against the white pillowcase. Flames. Sleep was taking over again. Lurking beyond the edge of sleep, she could feel the fires waiting in dreams for her. She didn't want any more fire.

"No more dreams. Please. No more." The other girl went back to the computer. Jan watched as the girl's fingers moved on the keyboard, quiet keyclicks in the stillness. The blue washed out of the screen again.

Blue. Lovely, cool blue. Jan closed her eyes, hugging the blue around her. She could feel it *washing over her like a wave, putting out the flames her hair made against the pillow, putting out the flames that lurked in her dreams.*

Jan slept.

SIX

When Jan woke up, she was thinking about the ocean. Her family had vacationed in California when she was fourteen, and she'd fallen in love with the Pacific. For once Jan wished she could remember a dream. Dreaming about the ocean would be a nice change.

Considering how much her arm hurt, it was surprising she hadn't had a nightmare. The pain medication had worn off, leaving Jan with the familiar cobwebby feeling in her mind and screaming pain where the scar tissue had been cut away the day before. This was the second time she'd gone in for what the plastic surgeon called "scar revision," and it hurt as much as it had the first time. The thought of going through several more years of treatment was depressing.

Aunt Leah had fixed a tray for Jan's breakfast, and Andrea brought it in before she left for school. "How're you feeling this morning?" she asked. Andrea looked tired.

"My arm hurts," Jan said. The contents of the tray amazed her. "Wow, French toast. Your mom's really pampering me." She took a sip of orange juice. "Not even any of that lousy tea."

Andrea shrugged. "It tastes awful, but Mom says it works."

"I don't see how you've been able to stand it."

"I'm used to it," she said. "I didn't expect you to be awake, after being up last night."

"Was I up?" The orange juice suddenly tasted as bitter as the tea. "I don't remember it."

"You came in and talked to me for a while," Andrea said. "I wanted to get to sleep; *I* have to go to school today. You didn't make much sense, if you want to know the truth." Andrea went through the bathroom to her own room, still talking. "Just rambling on about what the Foote place used to look like, and something about the library." She came back in with her knapsack. "Speaking of libraries, your books are due. Want me to drop them off and pick up your assignments?"

"Yeah, I guess," Jan said. "Although I don't think I'll do much today." She took another bite of French toast. It was starting to get cold.

"Work on it tomorrow, then. I've got to get moving, I'm late." Andrea shoved the library books in her bag and left for school.

Jan spent most of that day and the next in a haze of pills and pain. She did wake up when Julie and Barb stopped by after school the following day. They brought the week's edition of the *Cat Claws* and sat on the end of her bed, giving her an update on school gossip. But not all of it. They didn't repeat any of the gossip about Jan.

". . . and Sharon had to sit there and pretend she hadn't said a *word* about it, and Jack kept asking how we found out," Barb finished. "We were all just about choking, and he kept getting madder and madder. . . ."

"Sharon'd better watch it, or she's going to need a new boyfriend," Julie added.

Jan was so hazy, she couldn't focus on what they were saying. Instead she changed the subject. "Did Christy ever finish that article on Old Kenowa for Mr. Buehler?"

"She gave up on that ages ago," Julie said, looking at Jan oddly. "It needed photos of the Foote place, and now, of course, she can't get them."

"It's a shame," Barb said. "I was going to take the pictures for her, and now there aren't any buildings that old left in town. The Footes' was the last one, after . . ." She broke off, flushing. The only other house from that era had been Jan's. "The ones I took after the fire are pretty good, but they aren't what Christy needed."

"Oh," Jan said lamely. "Sorry, I forget stuff when I'm on pain medicine."

"Were you taking it at the slumber party?" Julie asked, her eyes narrowed. Jan shook her head.

"They don't give that junk to people until *after* they hurt, not before," Barb said practically. "I'll bet it hurts right now, doesn't it, Jan? We'd better let you sleep some more." She stood up. "Come on, Julie."

"You go on, I'll catch up in a minute," Julie said. "I want to ask Jan something private."

Barb closed the door behind her, and Julie turned back to Jan. "Jan, *did* you take anything that night?" she asked. "I've been wondering.

The *Chronicle* says the fire was set on purpose, and you acted so weird."

"I was just sleepwalking," Jan said.

"Yeah, but . . . I haven't told anyone," Julie said abruptly. "I promised. Only if anything else weird happens, I may break my promise. Just so you know." She left without another word.

Jan lay back against the pillow and closed her eyes. She thought of a bumper sticker she'd seen a few times. "Of all the things I've lost, I miss my mind the most." The first time she'd seen it, she'd laughed. It was supposed to be funny. People joked about losing their minds and going crazy all the time. But it had ceased being funny for Jan the first time she'd realized she might actually be losing hers.

When she had been in the hospital after the fire, the doctors told her it was normal to feel guilty for surviving, and that she shouldn't feel responsible for her parents' deaths. No one could figure out how she'd escaped. Her parents had died in their sleep, but Jan had always had a feeling that her mother had awakened her. It was impossible; her mother had probably been dead by then.

Now Jan was afraid she hadn't been asleep at

all. She'd once read about something called multiple personalities, people whose minds created other identities, completely different from each other. One "person" would do something, and the other parts of the mind wouldn't even know about it. She hadn't thought she was crazy, and the daytime Jan wasn't. Only what if there was another Jan?

That night Jan woke up abruptly, stumbling forward. She was at the top of the staircase. Instinctively her hands grabbed for the banisters. For a moment she hung supported on stiff arms, as though the railings were parallel bars. Jan straightened up carefully. Still grasping the banisters tightly, she sank back onto a step and sat there.

She'd walked in her sleep again, and this time she'd almost fallen down the stairs. That had never happened before. Although carpeted, they were long and steep; she could have been hurt badly. What was worse, she wasn't sure it was an accident. She had been going forward much too hard, as though she'd been pushed or had thrown herself toward the fall.

Jan got up carefully and quietly crept back up the stairs. When she got to her room, she wasn't surprised that her computer was on, even though she hadn't used it at all that day. Wearily she turned it off and got into bed. She hoped she'd stay there this time. As she dozed off, the thought crossed her mind that it might have been better if she *had* fallen down the steps and broken her neck. She doubted if she'd sleepwalk then.

When she woke up in the morning, both of her arms were aching, and the scars were throbbing in pain. Landing on her outstretched arms had jolted them; she was paying for it in additional soreness.

Jan returned to school for the first time in over a week. When she got there, she checked on makeup work for her morning classes. Dully she wondered if it was worth the bother. It would take a lot of effort to salvage the semester at this point, and she was afraid she wouldn't be there for the end of the school year anyway. Things couldn't go on another two months the way they had been.

Lunch arrived, but her usual haven was closed. Mr. Buehler was out for the day, and the substitute had locked the door to the newspaper room before going to the teachers' lunchroom. Mike and Julie were standing by the door when she got there.

"Didn't anyone tell the sub to leave it open?" she asked.

"I did, but she told me she wasn't going to leave a room open with all this computer equipment in it," Mike said. "I told her we'd be responsible, but I guess that wasn't good enough."

"I can't blame her," Julie said. Her mother was a sub as well. "Mr. Buehler's a nice guy, and he knows we don't trash the place, but the sub's new. My mom's had some real grief when kids messed stuff up, and the regular teachers got snotty."

"Yeah, but it means we're stuck eating in the lunchroom," Jan said.

The chatter in the cafeteria died away momentarily as the three sat down, then it resumed as loud as ever. *They were probably talking about me*, Jan thought. She'd always laughed at herself for thinking that way, but these days she was probably right.

Near the end of the lunch hour, there was a lull in the normal cafeteria noises.

"I still haven't said anything to anyone, Jan,"

Julie said quietly. "Since there haven't been any more fires, I don't think I'll have to."

It wasn't an accusation, it was an assumption of Jan's guilt. And she didn't believe Julie, anyway. Someone had started those rumors.

"Do you mean that if someone sets a fire, you'll tell everyone I did it?" Jan immediately regretted the question, but it was too late.

Julie's lips tightened. "I don't know," she said. "I guess it'll depend on whether or not someone sees you walking around it in the middle of the night, Jan."

There were a dozen kids gathered around their table listening to the argument, but Jan hardly noticed them. All of her tension and guilt and pain were being transformed into anger, directed at Julie. "Have you decided I started the fire? Did you see me lighting matches, or do you just think I did it because I was there? You were there too, you know!"

"At least I knew I was there," Julie snapped back. "You were asleep, you said."

"I didn't just say it!" Jan's voice rose, out of control. "You know I was sleepwalking!"

"All I know," Julie yelled, "is that the fires stopped when you were too sick to get out of bed. I wonder if they'll start again now."

Mike tried to get them both to stop shouting, but it was too late. By the time the crowd around them gave way reluctantly to Miss Pergondie, the damage was done. Anyone in the school who hadn't known about Jan's problems would now.

The economics teacher hauled them both off to the principal's office. Mr. Kahn was called in, as he always was for disciplinary matters. He looked at Jan sadly, which triggered her temper once more. Damn it, did he think she *wanted* to blow her senior year? She had no control over what was happening.

At least Julie didn't go into details over what had started the fight. Most of the student body might know the rumors, but no one had told the principal. From the look on Mr. Kahn's face, though, he'd heard them. Jan mumbled her way through a vague apology, and they were dismissed with a warning. Before Jan could escape, the counselor spoke. "Jan, since you're here anyway, I need to speak with you."

"Jan, it's getting worse," Mr. Kahn started when they got back to his office. "A lot of the kids talk to me, and I know you're still having problems. I suggested once before you should talk to someone about it. I'm going to repeat

93

that. You really should find someone who can help you."

She didn't think anyone could, but she didn't say so. After several more minutes during which Jan said nothing at all, he sighed again.

"In the meantime, your grades have slipped even more. You're failing in three classes, Jan. You never got below a C before this year. I know grades are probably the least of your worries right now, but I'm afraid you can't work on the *Claws* until they come up. I don't make the rules, and I wish I could bend this one, but the newspaper's counted as an extracurricular activity. I'm sorry."

"Like that's really going to help!" Jan shouted. "The only thing I'm any good at, and I have to stop doing it so I can do more of the stuff I'm lousy at?"

The sympathetic look on his face cooled her off slightly. "Look, I said it wasn't my idea, Jan. If it helps any, I agree with you. But neither of us can change the rules."

That was the end of it. Jan went back to class, still seething about the stupidity of it all. By the time she got home that night, she was ready to quit school the next day. The principal had called Aunt Leah, and the lectures went on until bedtime. There was no place she could go to get away from them. Aunt Leah and Uncle Peter were her guardians and trustees, and she was still under eighteen. She was stuck.

Mr. Kahn stretched, arching his back to get the kinks out. He was spending another late night at the school, trying to catch up on the paperwork that sometimes made him wish he were in a different line of work. He poured himself another cup of hot coffee from his thermos, then glanced at the clock on the wall. Almost midnight already. He'd finish this last file and call it quits for the night.

The counselor worked steadily for the next twenty minutes, his head bent. The papers on his desk almost hid a large framed photo of his wife. The Kahns had never had children; he figured he had a fresh set of several hundred each year. For the most part, once they left Central High, he never heard from them again. Occasionally, though, one would stop back and thank him. That made all the tedious paperwork worthwhile.

He finished updating the last record in the file and put away the folders. He was worried about Janelle Scott. There was more going on there than just prolonged grief for her family. He wished she'd go see some professional who could help her. He knew her aunt, though. It was unlikely she'd ever permit it.

Mr. Kahn flipped off the light and locked the door. He stretched again and started for the side entrance he always used at night, then paused. There was a dim light shining at the end of the hall, where the new wing joined the main corridor. He walked down the hall toward the light.

It was coming from the journalism classroom. The door to the room was open a crack. He reached the door and froze. He could smell something, a familiar smell—gasoline.

He spotted the source, and the small hairs on his neck stood up in a primitive reflex as he realized what it meant. He hurried across the room. A pile of printout paper, floppy disks, rags from the janitor's closet, and trash had been dumped beneath the long wooden table against the far wall. The pile was wet, reeking of gasoline. Balanced carefully on the edge of the table was a box of wooden matches, with a lit cigarette propped in the open end of the box.

Mr. Kahn snatched the cigarette, carefully moving over to the door to extinguish it. Whoever had set this up hadn't just wanted to start a small fire; this could bring down the entire school. And whoever it was couldn't be far away. Only a third of the cigarette was gone. He set the box of matches down on the nearest desk and looked around the room.

There was no one there. But the arsonist had to be someplace close. The counselor walked down the rows of desks, checking. As he reached the far side of the room, there was a faint creak behind him. He whirled. The door to the photography darkroom was open, and he was sure it had been closed before. Mr. Kahn headed for the door; he was going to put a stop to these fires right now. He yanked it open. The darkroom was empty.

As he took a step into the small room, someone thrust a garbage can violently into his side and shoved him, pushing hard against the small of his back. He sprawled forward, tripping from the unexpected attack, as a figure darted past him and slammed the door shut.

The sudden and total dark jarred him as badly as the fall. He got to his feet, stumbling over the trash can that was now rolling around, and made his way to the door. He flipped the light switch, but nothing happened. Even the special darkroom lights remained off. He tried to open the door, but it was locked. That didn't surprise him. He tried ramming it the way people always did on television shows, but all he did was hurt his shoulder.

He slid down and sat on the floor, his back against the storage cabinets. He was trapped; all he could do was wait for school the next day. The firebug had had plenty of time to escape. The first indication the counselor had that the arsonist hadn't left immediately was the faint smell of burning tobacco.

He scrambled clumsily to his feet, banging his hip against the cabinet. Another cigarette . . . The fuse of cigarette and matches must have been reset. He waited in the dark for an interminable time, then felt a jolt and heard a small *whoomp* on the other side of the locked door. The pile of gasoline-soaked materials under the table had caught fire.

In desperation he tried breaking down the door again. It was no use. He pulled his shirt over his head and lay down on the floor, hoping for a current of clean air. Smoke had started to ooze in around the door. It was growing harder to breathe, even near the floor. Mr. Kahn coughed, trying to keep his head down, as the fumes made him gag. Burning plastics, the carpets, printing chemicals . . .

He slowly drew himself up to his knees to check the door, feeling as high as he could reach without standing. He immediately snatched his hand back; the door was too hot to touch. As he slid back to the floor, fighting for breath, he heard the school's fire alarm through the door. The fumes were thickening.

The counselor passed out, overcome at last. Faint in the distance, sirens woke Kenowa once more.

SEVEN

The family was eating breakfast the next morning when they heard the news on the radio. *"Locally, fire claimed the life of the guidance counselor of Kenowa Central High School late last night, when a blaze of undetermined origin swept through the new wing of the school building. The body of Stephen Kahn, forty-seven, was found in the rubble of the journalism classroom. . . ."*

Jan dropped her spoon, upsetting her bowl of cereal, and Andrea shrieked, *"No!"* and fled from the table. While Aunt Leah cleaned up the mess, Jan sat motionless, not wanting to believe the news. The report went on to say that arson was suspected and the police were treating it as murder. The announcer closed with the brief statement that classes would meet, but that school would be dismissed early.

At that, Jan roused herself slightly. "I'm not going to school." She braced herself for a battle.

"Jan, I know it's not easy, but you can't afford to miss any more classes. You're going to go to school." Aunt Leah's tone was as sweet as ever, but there was steel under the sugarcoating. "Peter, go tell Andrea to behave herself and come finish her breakfast." Uncle Peter nodded once, then picked up his coffee cup again before heading upstairs to face his daughter.

"Aunt Leah, I am not going to go," Jan insisted. Go spend the day in a building stinking of fire, of death? "I don't care what you say. And I'll bet a lot of other kids won't go either. Mr. Kahn *died*, Aunt Leah!"

"I heard the news, Jan. I realize it's not easy for you to accept, but . . ."

"Not easy to accept!" Jan stood, shoving back her chair so hard, it almost tipped over. "I don't think you realize *anything*, I don't think you ever feel anything!" Her eyes were burning with tears she wouldn't let herself shed. "Do you want me to *accept* what happened to Mom and Dad, like it was no big deal? I'm surprised

101

you didn't make me go to school the day after . . ." She couldn't go on.

"Don't you dare talk to us that way!" Uncle Peter yelled. He raised his voice so seldom that Jan was silenced for a moment. "Your father was my brother. I miss him as much as you do!"

"I know, Uncle Peter." Jan could feel the tears forcing their way out. "I'm sorry, I didn't mean that, but I *won't* go to school and listen to everyone talking about Mr. Kahn and fires all day. I can't. *I just can't!*"

Aunt Leah spoke firmly, only a faint pursing of her lips showing her anger. "You may have been fond of Mr. Kahn, but you can't compare this to what happened to your parents."

"But it *is* the same, it's another fire, another damned fire . . ."

"Go or stay home, I don't care," Uncle Peter said. He stood abruptly. "Just stop talking about it!" He left, slamming the door so hard that the dishes rattled on the table.

"I hope you're satisfied," Aunt Leah said. "After all your uncle has done for you, and you treat him that way!"

"You were the one acting as though it didn't matter," Jan said. "I'm going upstairs." She started to cry as soon as she was out of the kitchen.

A little while later she heard the car pull out. Aunt Leah was driving Andrea the short distance to school. Jan watched as they drove away. Once they were out of sight, she turned away from the window and flipped on the radio. She wanted music, but the hourly news update was on. Jan turned the radio off again. She'd find out what had happened later, but right now she couldn't bear to listen.

Jan stayed in her room all day, thinking about the fire. She couldn't remember having been out of bed the night before, and there wasn't anything to indicate she'd been sleepwalking. Besides, the report on the radio said the fire had been started inside the building by someone who'd broken in through a window. She was positive she couldn't have done anything like that in her sleep. And she *knew* she wouldn't have hurt Mr. Kahn.

A part of Jan was still afraid that she was crazy, but another part denied the possibility. Even madness must have some limits. But if she wasn't doing it, who was, and why had she been at the Blue Willow? Maybe the arsonist was someone she knew and cared about, and she was aware of it only in her sleep. She flopped down across her bed, hugging the stuffed cat that Mike had given her, and tried to figure out what had been going on in Kenowa for the last two months.

Jan was still lying in bed thinking when her cousin got home from school. Andrea's eyes were red, and she slammed her door and locked it, refusing to talk to Jan or Aunt Leah or, when the phone rang, any of her friends. She didn't blame Andrea; Jan didn't want to talk to anyone herself. For a while she answered the phone, but she soon got tired of trying to change the subject. She gave up, copying Andrea and letting the phone ring until her aunt answered. After the fourth call, Aunt Leah unplugged the phone and there was silence.

Jan didn't refuse to see Mike, though, when he stopped by around four o'clock. She came down to meet him in the family room. As soon as Aunt Leah left them, Jan moved into his embrace. They stood there for several long minutes, not saying anything, just clinging to each other.

Finally he broke the clinch. "Are you all right?" he demanded. "I saw Andrea today. She said you had a fight with your aunt over not coming to school."

She nodded. "I couldn't face everyone talking. How're the kids taking it?"

"They're mad," Mike said. "I mean, yeah, they're upset, and a lot of kids were crying, but everyone's angry. Even the jerks knew better than to make any cracks about what happened." He sat down on the end of the couch and stared up at her. His expression bothered Jan; she couldn't read it. "You don't joke about murder."

"Do they always call it murder when someone gets killed in an arson fire?" she asked, sitting down on the arm of the sofa beside him.

"Not always," Mike said. "Mr. Kahn was inside the darkroom and the door was locked. From outside. Someone had to have locked him in before the fire was set." The expression on Mike's face was still unreadable.

"Oh, no." It was more a moan than words.

"Deliberate murder," Mike went on. "They figure he must have seen something, because normally he wouldn't have been there at all. So he saw something, or someone thought he did, and whoever it was made sure he couldn't get away." Mike paused. "They didn't find him at first, you know. The fire fighters weren't expecting anyone to be there at that hour, so they didn't search that much. They didn't start looking for him until Mrs. Kahn showed up. She was worried because he wasn't home yet."

Jan shut her eyes, wishing she could shut off her imagination as easily as she could her vision. She'd met Mrs. Kahn a few times. In her mind Jan could see her, glancing at the clock, fretting about the time, hearing the sirens, standing there while the fire fighters searched through the blazing building. . . .

"Who could *do* something like that?" Jan demanded. She'd asked herself that question a hundred times.

"A lot of people have been asking that," Mike said. "And a few of them think they know."

Something in his voice made her open her eyes again. He was staring at her, the expression on his face completely blank. Wordlessly he held out a slim book. It was torn and filthy, the cover ripped half-off, and the pages soggy. Jan took it, recognizing it immediately. It was a book of poetry Mike had given her shortly after they'd started dating. Now it was ruined. Jan could smell the smoke on it.

"I picked it up outside what's left of the

Claws office," he said quietly. "How did it get there, Jan?"

"I don't know," she said. "Do you think . . . Mike, what *are* you thinking? Do you think I started that fire?"

"I don't want to think so," he said, looking away. He sounded tired. "But with everything else that's been going on, do you blame me for wondering?"

She couldn't; she'd wondered herself. "I liked Mr. Kahn."

"So did everybody else. Someone still killed him."

There was nothing she could say. She offered no excuses, except, "I didn't do it."

"Are you sure?" Mike asked. "Could you— Jan, I don't want to ask this, but I have to. Could you have done it in your sleep?"

"No!" All of the questions she'd been asking herself all day long boiled out; she told him of her doubts about her own sanity, her nightmares, her conviction that no matter what, she couldn't have done something like that without being aware of it. When she finished, she was physically exhausted and drained of emotion.

Mike slipped his arm around her waist. "All right. But if you didn't do it . . ."

"I know," she said irritably. "If I didn't, who did?"

Neither spoke for several minutes. Jan turned her face, pressing it against Mike's chest. It felt good just to be with him. For the moment he seemed to accept her denial.

"The *Claws* is out of business for a while," he said, changing the subject. "The journalism room's totaled."

"Is there anything we can do?" she asked, forgetting for the moment that she was no longer permitted to work on the paper.

"It'll take us a week or so, but . . . yeah, we're going to keep going if we have to write it out by hand in crayon," Mike said, positively. "I was wondering, can we use your computer?"

"Sure. Only," she added, "I can't help you with it. Not officially, anyway." The previous afternoon felt several lifetimes away. She had to explain the problem with her grades to him. She finished up with, "And no, I still didn't set the fire. I love the *Cat Claws*. I'm not going to wreck it just because I'm not on it anymore!"

"I believe you, Jan," Mike said. He looked down at the sodden book on the end table. "I just hope that believing you isn't a mistake."

* * *

108

Shortly before supper, a pair of men rang the doorbell and asked to speak with Jan. One was a plainclothes policeman. The other was an arson investigator from the State Fire Marshal's Office, named Randall. Jan had met Inspector Randall before, during the investigation into the fire that had killed her parents. Inevitably someone had mentioned the rumors about her to the police.

Jan led them into the family room, glad that she'd taken the poetry book up to her own room after Mike had left. Its connection to the fire would have been too obvious. Aunt Leah hovered in the doorway while the men spoke with Jan.

"Miss Scott, can you tell us about the fight you had yesterday with Mr. Kahn, the counselor at your school?" Randall asked.

"What fight?" Jan asked, taken off guard. "I liked Mr. Kahn, I didn't have a fight with him!"

"I'm afraid that's not what the school secretary reported," Randall said. "According to her, you were told that you had to drop certain extracurricular activities, including journalism, and you got upset. She said you were shouting."

Jan shied away from remembering the scene, but she had definitely shouted. She said so, but added, "But I know it wasn't Mr. Kahn's fault. He just told me about it."

"It wouldn't be the first time someone got blamed for delivering bad news," he said. Without giving her a chance to respond to this, he said, "Can you tell me about these memory problems you've been having lately? Who's your doctor? Are you being treated for somnambulism?"

Jan answered as well as she could. As she spoke, she repeated in her mind the arguments she'd had with herself that day. She couldn't have set all of those fires. She might have some problems, but she wasn't a murderer. Her belief in herself weakened as he continued to probe. From some of the questions, it was obvious that Julie had definitely broken her promise. They knew all about the slumber party, her reaction to the video—and her presence at the Blue Willow fire. Well, Julie had warned Jan she'd tell if anything else happened.

They went over the same ground again and again, until Jan was ready to scream. Then they shifted the focus to the fire seven months before. Jan knew they'd never decided what had caused it, but she hadn't realized it was still an open case. Now she discovered she was under suspicion, as a result of the recent events. They asked to see the scars on her arms, and made a note of the name of her plastic surgeon.

While Inspector Randall carefully examined her arm, Jan asked, "Do you really think I'd burn myself like this on purpose? No one could; it hurts too much."

"Not on purpose, no. But a lot of firebugs manage to catch themselves." He looked up and met her eyes. "Can you tell us how you got out of your house, Miss Scott?"

"I told you before, I can't remember!" Jan snapped, her temper fraying.

They quickly went back to discussing the fire at the school. Jan did learn a few things she hadn't known, and one of them bothered her. They asked her if she had keys to the journalism room. A broken window had been only the first step in getting into the school and setting the fire. The door of the newspaper room had been opened with a key.

Jan told them that she didn't have those keys and never had. It was true. But she knew who did.

The editor of the *Claws*. Mike had an extra set of keys.

* * *

At dinner that evening Jan had no appetite. She sat there listening to Aunt Leah tell Uncle Peter all about the interrogation. Halfway through the meal, Andrea joined them. It was only the second time Jan had seen her cousin since breakfast. She'd seen Andrea briefly when she'd arrived home from school, before she'd locked herself in her room. Her eyes had been red then. Now they were even redder, and puffy and swollen. She sat without eating, until her mother said sharply, "Andrea, the idea of supper is eating."

"Leave her alone!" Jan said in defense of her cousin. "You made her go to school, that's bad enough. It must have been horrible." She glared at her aunt defiantly. "Maybe Andrea shouldn't obey your orders all the time the way she does. You aren't always right!"

For the second time that day, Andrea fled the table in tears. Aunt Leah returned Jan's glare and said venomously, "She's a good girl. And at least Andrea hasn't ever tried to kill me." She left the room, leaving Jan shaken. Did everyone think Jan was a murderer?

* * *

Jan woke up several times during the night, with nightmares that left her screaming in her sleep. After the last one, she turned on the lamp by her bed and left it on. She hoped the comfort of a simple electric light would keep images of the dead guidance counselor from haunting her dreams.

She dozed fitfully for a long time, finally slipping into deep sleep. The next thing she knew, she was awake, her feet cold. She looked around.

She was standing in the hall, in front of the open door of the house. Something was in her hand, and she looked down, knowing what it was before she saw it. An open cardboard box of wooden matches.

"No!" She threw the box down the front steps, matches spraying across the lawn. "Do you hear me, I said *no*! I don't believe this. Stop doing this to me, whoever you are!"

There was no one around. She was shouting at an empty street. But she could feel another presence. And Jan meant what she'd said. She hadn't hurt Mr. Kahn, she *couldn't* have. In the back of her mind, she could hear her mother's voice whispering, *"Believe in yourself, Jan, always believe in yourself."*

113

She was going to believe in herself, not in the lie of that box of matches. She slammed the door shut, sending echoes down the street as she returned to bed.

EIGHT

Jan skipped school again the next day. She didn't feel like having another fight with Aunt Leah, so she set her alarm clock for half an hour earlier than usual. Getting out of bed was almost impossible, and Jan remembered she'd been sleepwalking again. She felt exhausted. And waking up this early made it worse. But it was worth it to sneak out of the house without a fuss.

She showered quickly, then got dressed and slipped out the back door without breakfast. She was gone at least fifteen minutes before her aunt would expect her for breakfast. She left a note on the kitchen table, telling them what she was doing. She was free—at least for the day. The state capital was a little over an hour away;

Jan steered her car toward the open road and stepped on the gas.

Jan drove to a mall in the capital and spent an hour shopping, trying on clothes just for something to do. It wasn't much fun all by herself, though, and she knew she was trying to keep from thinking. It was like a joke Mike had told her once, when he'd solemnly suggested she *not* think of a purple plush rabbit. Of course, trying not to think about something meant her mind was focused entirely on that thing. It had been funny, trying to keep her mind off Easter baskets and stuffed animals while they hopped through her thoughts. Trying not to think about Mr. Kahn, or fires, or sleep-walking and nightmares, was just as futile, but not nearly as pleasant.

The mall wasn't much good as a distraction, so she went on into downtown Springfield and joined some tourists visiting Abe Lincoln's home. Jan had been there so many times, she could have replaced the guide. She walked a few blocks down to the Capitol building and wandered around for a while, but the legislature wasn't in session, and all she really saw were more tourists. Despite the presence of the state government, Springfield wasn't an exciting city. She treated herself to lunch in a steak house, then started back, tape player blasting at full volume.

Rather than going straight home, Jan drove over to the library. Some reading might help to distract her, and maybe she could check out that psych book on sleepwalking. She found several novels she thought might hold her attention, but the book that explained sleepwalking was gone, as were several others in that section. Jan recalled a book on multiple personalities; it, too, was missing. Those that were left were uniformly dull, loaded with jargon and mystifying charts. Someone had checked out all of the readable texts. Jan went to the desk to ask about them.

"What? No, that book should be on the shelf." The library aide sounded positive. Jan gave her another reference number, and the aide pulled it up on the computer. "Nope, that one's there, too. Are you sure you were checking the right section?"

"Yes, I'm sure, and the books aren't there," Jan said. She checked out her novels and went home. It was well after dark; at least there wouldn't be much time for a fight.

Aunt Leah met her as she came in the back

117

door. "And just where have you been all day?" she demanded.

"Springfield," Jan said. "I didn't want to go to school." She headed for the kitchen, her aunt following as the lecture began. Aunt Leah had plenty to say about Jan's ditching school and driving off without a word.

Jan opened the refrigerator, which sidetracked her aunt for a moment. "Haven't you eaten?" she asked. "Here, let me." She pushed Jan aside and got out several covered plastic dishes with leftovers from the evening meal. "We have a regular mealtime, you know. It's common courtesy to be here on time for supper. . . ." The microwave made reheating the food a simple job, but Aunt Leah managed to make it sound like a major chore. As soon as Jan sat down to eat, the lecture veered back to the original subject. "It's not as though your grades are so high these days that you can just skip school whenever you want to. . . ."

At last Aunt Leah ran down, and Jan finished her meal in peace. Climbing the stairs, Jan was sure she hadn't heard the end of it, but the day had been worth a few lectures. She got ready for bed, making sure the alarm was set for the same early hour. She planned on ditching again.

She'd go back to school next week, maybe. Or the week after. Maybe. Or maybe not.

"Jan, sit up. Sit up, Jan. Jan . . ." The voice was soft but insistent, as was the gentle shaking. "Jan, sit up and take your medicine." She sat up and took the white tablet from Andrea. There was a glass of water in her hand already. Strange, she didn't remember asking for any medicine.

"Didn't I already take this?" Everything was sleep-fogged, but she was sure Andrea had given her the pain medicine earlier. "I don't hurt anymore, honest."

"Take the medicine, Jan. You need to take it."

The tablet went down with a gulp of water. Another materialized in her hand, and she stared at it. Hadn't she stopped taking these? But she felt sleepy, and it wasn't worth arguing about.

In the otherwise darkened room, a figure sat at the computer, pecking hesitantly at the keys. In the bed on the other side of the room, Jan slept heavily, her breathing labored.

* * *

119

"Jan, get up. Let me help you." Jan got out of the bed under the gentle urging, staggering slightly.

"I'm tired. I'm so tired, let me go back to bed. . . ."

"In a minute, Jan." Andrea helped her into the chair in front of the computer. Gentle blue light washed over her from the monitor. "Touch the keys, Jan. Touch them. . . ." She could feel her hands being guided to the keys, but they were remote, not part of her. Fingers gently pushed down on her own fingers, pressing them against the keys.

"The keyboard doesn't work," Jan said. The fingers pressed Jan's fingers against the keys, but new words didn't form. Her eyes tried to focus on the white letters already on the screen, but the words didn't make sense. Something about death, and fire, and her parents. "I don't want to type, I want to sleep. . . ."

"In a minute." Jan's hands were guided to touch the power switch, the monitor, the mouse. "Now, back to bed." She leaned heavily against Andrea as they moved across the room. Sitting heavily on the edge of the bed, she felt dizziness washing over her like a wave. Waves of blue *from the computer. She'd dreamed about them before.*

"Take this." A hard cylinder was pressed into her hands, then another. With difficulty, she focused on it. A prescription medicine bottle. The last fell from her hands as her grasp slackened and she fell onto her side. Sleepy, she was so sleepy. . . .

The soft blue light from the screen was the only light in the room. Jan slept, her breathing ragged. Someone approached the bed. The figure reached out to the unconscious girl and shook her shoulder gently.

"Jan, take your medicine. Please take your medicine. . . ."

She couldn't sit up, she was too sleepy. Water slopped down the front of her nightgown, cold and shocking, as she gagged on the capsule. Her stomach hurt. "Please, no more." For a moment, nausea overwhelmed her.

"You have to take the medicine, Jan, you want to die. Don't you remember? You want to join your parents. . . ."

Her parents. Jan remembered her parents, her father, who was never too busy for a joke, her

121

mother and her enthusiasm for books and the lives of people long since gone. History. Her mother was history now, because she wasn't here anymore. She remembered thinking it would be easy to join them, to be dead with them.

She took the last capsule and fell back against the pillows. Now she could sleep.

But why was Andrea crying?

Before Jan opened her eyes, she heard a soft, whispery hiss and a bubbling noise. The back of her throat felt raw. She tried to open her eyes, but they seemed to be glued shut. She tried again, and they opened reluctantly, as the mucus sealing them gave way. A smooth white ceiling with a set of metal tracks embedded in it was above her. She tried to turn her head.

As she did, the rest of the room came into focus. It was a strange room, pale beige walls, a television on a metal crane jutting from one, a window with the blinds adjusted to keep out the light. A hospital room; why was she in the hospital?

As she tried to figure that out, Jan became aware of other things. Her muscles felt stiff, as though she'd spent too much time in one posi-

122

tion. She was tethered to the wall by an oxygen tube, clamped to her nose. That was the bubbling sound and hiss. The air ran through a bubbler, adding moisture to it, and the nosepiece didn't fit quite right. The inside of her nose felt dry, as if the skin were going to crack. And her throat felt as though someone had been using a paint scraper inside it.

"Well, you're awake. How do you feel?" Jan turned her head toward the strange voice, which sounded professionally cheerful. Her eyes focused on the figure beside her. She was not surprised to see a nurse; the voice and question had sounded like a hospital nurse. Jan fought down a moment's panic. Had Uncle Peter and Aunt Leah's house burned down as well?

"My throat hurts," Jan whispered. It came out like a croak.

"I don't doubt it," the nurse said. "You've had tubes down it; they always hurt. It should feel better in a few days." Jan looked past the uniform to see the woman wearing it. The nurse was young, with concern and humor visible in her expression. "Want to sit up a little?" Jan nodded. There was a faint electric whine as the nurse raised the head of the bed slightly. "You tell me if you get dizzy, or if it gets to be too tiring. After a while we'll see if you're up to a little walk to the bathroom."

Jan felt as though she'd never have enough strength to get up again. Even leaning back, she felt too weak to move. "Why am I here?" she asked. "What happened? Was there an accident?"

The humor vanished from the nurse's face. "Can't you remember?" Jan shook her head, and the nurse probed. "Anything at all? What's the last thing you *do* remember?"

"Going to bed," Jan said. "Aunt Leah was mad because I ditched school. Is she all right? Did anything happen?"

"Your family is fine," the nurse said briefly, "but I don't think I'd better say anything else right now. The doctor will be here shortly." She looked past the head of the bed at something and added, "I'll be right back. Don't try to get up. If you need someone before then, the call button is there on the right." She picked up a clipboard and left the room.

Jan twisted around to see what the nurse had looked at. There were some monitors behind her, and she became aware for the first time that there were sensors taped to her arms and chest. Turning back around, she closed her eyes, as a faint dizziness made the room whirl around her. Get up, right. She'd collapse before she could get her feet over the side of the bed.

Jan couldn't remember anything beyond going to bed the night before. She shifted against the pillow uneasily. Had it only been the night before? By the time Dr. Holsinger came in, Jan was half crazy with frustration.

"How do you feel, Jan?" The doctor touched her forehead lightly, then looked at the monitors.

"I feel frustrated," Jan said flatly. "No one's told me a thing. Why am I in here?"

Dr. Holsinger looked tired. Her eyes fixed on Jan's face, she said quietly, "Jan, you tried to kill yourself. You almost succeeded."

"No . . ." It didn't make sense. The nightmares, the fires, now this. "No, I didn't! I don't remember it, I couldn't have!"

The doctor sighed. "To be frank, I'm not surprised you don't remember the attempt. You've had some memory blanks in the last month, haven't you?" She echoed Jan's hesitant nod. "And heavy barbiturates like the ones you took can cloud the mind even under normal conditions. It's why people often can't remember what happens the first few days after they have major surgery. You took a huge amount of codeine—your pain medication from the plastic surgery—all of the clonazepam for sleepwalking, some sleeping capsules I prescribed for your uncle after the fire . . ." She shook her head. "Quite honestly, I'm not sure how you survived. You've been unconscious for over thirty-six hours." Jan heard a faint whimper and realized it came from her. "We've had you on oxygen the whole time. We pumped your stomach, but too much of the drugs had been absorbed, so it was mainly a matter of watching you and being ready to restart your heart if it stopped." Dr. Holsinger looked grim. "It almost did, several times, yesterday. I don't think anyone can come closer to dying than you did."

"But I don't remember," Jan insisted, near tears.

"Perhaps that's just as well," Dr. Holsinger said gently. "Think of it as your mind calling for help. The blackouts and sleepwalking may have been also, but you didn't get the help you needed. Now maybe you will."

"Help?"

"Help in dealing with your parents' death.

All of this probably comes from never really accepting that they're gone."

Jan didn't answer. What the doctor said made sense, but it didn't account for the other things that had been happening. Unless the fires had been another call for help. But if that was the case, what about the fire that had taken her parents from her and started the entire thing?

Dr. Holsinger stood up. "Your family's outside. I called them when I got word you were awake, but I wanted to see you first. We'll talk more tomorrow."

A few minutes later, Aunt Leah and Uncle Peter came in. Andrea lingered in the door, but finally she joined them and took the chair near the foot of the bed.

"Well, Janelle," Aunt Leah began. "You've given everyone quite a bad scare."

"Leah," Uncle Peter cut in. "Give the girl a chance to get over it a little. Are you all right, Janny?"

Jan's throat tightened. Her father had always called her Janny, and no one else had used the name since his death. She nodded, unable to speak for a moment, then croaked, "My throat hurts."

"They let us in to see you a couple of times before," he said, "but you were always asleep. I'm glad you're finally awake."

"So am I, Uncle Peter." He squeezed her hand, and she felt a rush of affection for him. Jan realized for the first time that he loved her in his own way, very much.

"I am, too," Andrea said, her voice very low. As she said it, a tear dripped down her cheek.

"We all are, of course," Aunt Leah said impatiently, "but we can't ignore what happened. Jan, you should have told us about whatever had you so upset instead of trying to commit suicide."

"What did happen?" She still couldn't remember, and no one had really told her anything yet.

"We were hoping you could tell us, Janny," Uncle Peter said, clearing his throat. "I woke up a little early, and I saw a light from your room. Your computer was on. I read what was on the screen, and, well . . . it was close. Another ten minutes and I don't think we would have made it."

Jan felt a chill. *That close* . . . "Uncle Peter, what was on the computer? I don't get it."

"Your suicide note, Jan," Andrea said. "You

said you wanted to die and—and all sorts of things."

A foggy memory of sitting in front of the monitor late at night floated to the surface of Jan's mind. She could feel her fingers on the keys and see words on the screen about fire, and death. There was something else, something she couldn't remember. "What sort of things?"

"That you wanted to be with your parents," Andrea said, shakily.

Another cloudy memory forced its way into Jan's consciousness. *A white tablet in her hand. And almost choking on a capsule, gagging on the water as she forced it down* . . . Again there was something Jan knew was missing from the memory, but it didn't really matter. She had tried to kill herself. She couldn't deny it any longer. She sagged back, closing her eyes in defeat.

"I'm afraid that isn't all," her aunt said. Jan opened her eyes wearily. She didn't need anything else. She stiffened as Aunt Leah continued. "We haven't called the police about it, but I'm afraid we'll have to, sooner or later. Your note *rambled*, dear. It wasn't very clear, but it implied that you killed Mr. Kahn. And set the

fire that killed your parents, as well." Her aunt
exchanged a glance with Uncle Peter, then went
on quietly. "I'm not surprised you tried to kill
yourself."

NINE

Jan had plenty of time over the next two days to think about what her aunt had said. The memory of the suicide attempt remained vague, and she was sure she'd forgotten something important. But she could clearly see the white pills in her hand and feel the gag reflex as she swallowed, time after time. She couldn't recall actually writing the suicide note, but her fingers remembered the cool feel of the keys in the darkened room. No matter how impossible it seemed, she must have tried to kill herself.

But she couldn't have set fire to her own house. It was impossible—why would she have wanted to hurt her parents? She knew plenty of kids had trouble with their folks. Mike had constant battles with his stepfather, and Christy kept shuttling between her divorced parents. Some of Jan's other friends hadn't even seen one of their parents in several years. She had been one of the *lucky* ones, with parents who loved each other and her. Only a maniac would have given that up.

Which was what she was afraid she was—insane. She asked Dr. Holsinger the next time she came in if someone could go crazy without knowing it. The conversation didn't satisfy Jan's curiosity, since the doctor refused to say anything specific. Jan finally asked the doctor point-blank if she could have killed someone without remembering it, and why she would want to hurt those she loved. Dr. Holsinger didn't think Jan was mentally ill; she refused to use the word "crazy." But she emphasized that she wasn't an expert.

"Jan, I told you before that you needed some professional help," Dr. Holsinger said. She stood up to leave, as the nurse brought in the supper tray. "I'm going to speak with your aunt and uncle about getting you in to see a psychologist." She paused in the doorway. "For what it's worth, I don't think you hurt your parents. But we have to make sure now that you don't hurt yourself again."

She'd gone after that, leaving Jan to pick moodily at her supper. The hospital food was bland, and she still didn't have much appetite. *For what it was worth* . . . By her own admission, Dr. Holsinger's opinion wasn't worth much more than a layman's in a case like this.

Julie came to visit Jan the following afternoon. Julie treated Jan in a clumsy, "there, there, now" way that grated on Jan's nerves within three minutes. It sounded as if Julie were reading from a get-well card.

After five minutes of syrup, Jan's temper snapped. "C'mon, Julie, talk straight."

"What do you mean?" Cut off in midsentence, Julie sounded confused by Jan's demand.

"You think I've gone crazy. Maybe I have. But dammit, I can still think!" Jan's voice cracked slightly on the last word, as her sore throat started to ache again. Lowering her voice, she went on. "You've been talking to me like I was in kindergarten. The way adults without any brains talk to little kids. You know what I mean."

Julie's face was red, but she giggled slightly. "Yeah, I always wanted to stick my tongue out at them. I hated it when they patted me on the head."

"So did I." Jan grinned back at her. "And you've been patting me on the head since you walked in here. It feels that way, anyhow. Can't you just *talk* to me?"

"All right," Julie said. "What do you want to talk about?"

This was the hard part, but Jan wanted to know. "What are the kids saying at school?"

All traces of amusement fled from Julie's face. Slowly she said, "I could play games, but I won't. Most everyone thinks you've gone completely insane. A lot of them think . . ." She faltered, then plunged on. "Some of the kids say you set the fire at the school. That you murdered Mr. Kahn."

Jan leaned back against the pillows, staring at the white ceiling. That was it, then. Even if she wasn't crazy, no one would believe it. The verdict had been reached by her peers, the kids she'd known most of her life. "What do *you* think?" she asked. She kept her eyes on the meeting point of wall and ceiling, rather than looking at Julie.

"I don't know," Julie said hesitantly. "I don't *want* to believe it, but everyone knows you've

been having trouble, and you'd just been sus-
pended from the paper. . . ."

It was an honest answer.

"I told the police about the sleepwalking,"
she said, her voice so low that it was almost
inaudible. "I'm sorry, but I had to. When Mr.
Kahn . . . it was too serious."

"Yeah." Jan sighed. "Don't worry, Julie, you
did what you had to. I don't blame you, I probably would have myself. I just wish you hadn't
told anyone before that."

"Who said I had?" Julie asked, her voice
tight. "I promised that night. I said I wouldn't,
and I didn't."

There was a moment's silence. Then Jan said,
"Somebody did. There were rumors before
. . . Barb asked me about it less than two
weeks after the slumber party. I know you said
you didn't, but I figured you must have told at
least one other kid. Andrea swears she didn't
say anything."

"I don't break promises, and I don't lie," Julie said. She stood up to leave. "Maybe you told
someone yourself."

"Me?" Jan's eyes widened. "You think I'd tell
someone I was sleepwalking around fires?"

"You might have." Julie stared down at Jan

135

for a moment, then looked pointedly around the hospital room. "Can you really be sure of anything you've done, Jan?" She walked out, leaving Jan to answer the question to herself.

Mike came by that evening and sat beside the bed for a while, not saying much, just holding her hand. Her uncle Peter stopped in several times on his own, and a couple of times with Aunt Leah. Andrea showed up long enough to give her a card from some of her classmates. Only a couple of kids had signed it. Her cousin just muttered a few disjointed sentences and fled. Her eyes were red again, Jan noticed. Odd to think of Andrea being that upset over her. They'd never been that close. *Maybe she likes me better than I thought,* Jan mused.

It didn't bother Jan too much that the nurses were monitoring her closely. Jan talked to them when she could and kept the television on almost constantly, desperately flipping around the channels, looking for something interesting to watch. Quiz shows and soaps were useless, and sitcoms were almost as boring. A rerun of an old suspense movie managed to distract her for a while, but she got confused by the plot twists before it was half-over. She really wasn't paying attention.

While her eyes fixed, unseeing, on the film, Jan followed her thoughts to their unpleasant conclusion. She was sure she couldn't kill people, but people had died. She didn't remember attempting suicide, but she had. Even her friends and family thought she was guilty; it probably wouldn't be long before she was arrested. Maybe a court would decide she was innocent because she was insane. It certainly seemed that way.

That might satisfy the courts, but it wouldn't satisfy Jan. She'd never believed in the death penalty, but she was ready to impose it on herself. She still hadn't seen the suicide note, and no one had told her exactly what it said. There was just a hazy image in her mind of the blue screen in the dark room. But the part of her that had been starting fires had wanted to die. That might not be such a bad idea.

And this time, she wouldn't botch the job.

Jan went home three days after waking up. Dr. Holsinger looked grave and repeated her recommendation that Jan get some professional help, but she couldn't hold her in the hospital any longer against Aunt Leah's insistence that Jan would recover faster at home.

Her own bed did feel good. The computer in the corner taunted her silently, but she couldn't face it yet. She went to sleep easily, more easily than she had in the hospital, and passed the night dreamlessly.

It was Sunday. Between unconsciousness and the repetitive hospital routine, Jan had lost track of the days. She took her time with the Sunday paper, including sections she usually didn't bother reading. The family left her alone for the most part, but several times she glanced up to see Uncle Peter watching her. Each time he gave her a quick smile that was obviously meant to be reassuring. It wasn't; his worry was too visible beneath the surface. It was a relief when Mike showed up around one. Her uncle excused himself, leaving them alone together. Jan realized he'd been guarding her.

Mike hugged her, but he released her almost immediately. She felt a pang; *I don't blame him for not wanting to hug a murderer.* Even with Mike standing there beside her, she felt as lonely as she had in the hospital.

"How do you feel?" he asked her.

Jan said, "Fine," while thinking, *I tried to kill myself! How does he* think *I feel?*

Some trace of her thoughts must have shown on her face, because he said hastily, "Dumb question, sorry. I just wondered if your throat still hurt."

"Not as much," she said. In fact, her throat was almost back to normal by now, although she still had headaches. Dr. Holsinger had advised her to tough them out, without even an aspirin, for the same reason she hadn't allowed Jan any drugs at all while in the hospital. Until all the residue of what she'd taken was out of her system, it would be better not to add anything new to the mixture.

"Remember when I said we were going to keep the *Claws* going?" Mike asked, changing the subject. "You said we could use your computer. Is the offer still open?"

"Sure," Jan said, leading the way up to her room. She hadn't turned the computer on since she'd gotten home. She was afraid to read her suicide note. She had no problem with Mike using it, though.

Neither of them talked while Mike worked. In the past he would have told her about the articles, read snippets to her, asked her advice on a word choice or phrase. Now the silence was uncomfortable, and she jumped when he broke it.

"At least the editorial is done." He reached over to the printer beside the computer and flipped it on. As the printer clattered, he stood to one side, mutely offering Jan room to stand and read the output with him.

The editorial was a simple tribute to Mr. Kahn. Mike had skipped the obvious stuff, like his age and where he'd gone to school. Instead he'd focused on the difference the counselor had made to the students at Kenowa Central. Long before she reached the bottom of the page, Jan's eyes were filled with tears, making it impossible for her to read or even see the final sentences.

"That's wonderful, Mike," she whispered.

"It's lousy," he said, turning away from the computer in sudden anger. "Everybody's going to cry when they read it. Hell, I did when I wrote it. But having to write it was lousy. Why did it . . ." He broke off.

Why did it happen? she finished silently for him. She didn't know.

* * *

140

After Mike left, Jan sat down in front of the computer. She was ready to face whatever she found. Or she hoped she was.

She started by looking through the directory of files. There were several names she didn't recognize, all of which had time stamps indicating middle-of-the-night work. She called one up, grimly certain of what she'd see. As she expected, the file was filled with the same sort of ravings she'd seen before, choppy and almost incoherent. She didn't read it all. Fast checks of a few others revealed the same thing. She should have checked before now. Maybe if she had, she would have found some way to get help, and Mr. Kahn wouldn't have died. . . .

Yeah, right, she thought sourly. She had almost convinced herself last week she couldn't have done all these things. Her faith in herself had faded in the hospital bed, with the hazy memory of the pills she'd taken. She searched on through the other files.

Finally she found it. The note began, *The flames are dancing again, but I don't want to dance with them this time. Instead I will sleep* . . . As Aunt Leah had said, it rambled. There wasn't a clear-cut confession, but there was a great deal about her parents, and dancing flames, and death. Mr. Kahn was "the man who wanted to watch the dance." He'd been locked away so he couldn't. Toward the end, the note shifted tone, becoming almost coherent. As Andrea had said, it said in so many words, "I want to die. . . ."

There was no suggestion in the morning that Jan go to school. It would have been out of the question even if she hadn't had other plans. Andrea promised to say hi for her to everyone, which was amusing. By the time the hellos had been said, Jan would have said her final good-bye.

Uncle Peter left for work, and Aunt Leah began to gather her supplies together for her art class. "Now, are you sure you'll be all right here alone, Janelle?"

"Sure, I'm sure," Jan said.

"Well, if you're positive. . . . I hate to leave you, but this trip's been scheduled for a month." The portable easel went into the canvas bag as her aunt kept talking. "The gardens aren't open to regular tour groups, you know; we're really very fortunate that they decided to let our art club in for this sketching session, and the flowers are so beautiful right now. . . ."

142

With a start, Jan realized that for the last few weeks, she'd been so wrapped in misery and death that she'd missed the onset of spring. Early blossoms had given way to the hardier ones, and all the leaves were out on the trees by now. Anyone who could overlook an Illinois springtime in favor of death *must* be crazy.

It took another twenty minutes of fussing, but at last Aunt Leah left. Jan waited an extra fifteen minutes, in case her aunt had forgotten something and came back. This time Jan wanted no interruptions.

She went out to her car, which was parked in front of the house, and pulled it into the garage. Then she shut the door.

Jan couldn't face fire, and all the medicine was used up. Uncle Peter didn't keep guns, so that was out, and she shied away from the blood and pain of knives. But cars could be deadly weapons, too.

There were several piles of rags in the garage. Jan shoved them under the crack of the garage door and around the sides. Then she got out a roll of duct tape. She used the silvery tape to go along the bottom of the garage door; then she ran a line of tape up each side of the door, as high as she could reach. It wasn't a perfect seal, but Jan figured it would be good enough.

Her heart pounding, she suddenly ran back through the side door into the kitchen. The realization that this was it, that she was about to die, hit her full force. She started to shake so hard, she had to lean up against the counter, and for a moment she thought she was going to vomit. Waves of pure terror broke over her. No wonder she'd done it in her sleep that last time, she thought. It was a lot easier to kill yourself when you didn't have to think about what you were doing.

Several minutes passed before she could go on. Stepping over to the sink, she got a glass of water and drained it thirstily. Her throat was even drier than it had been in the hospital. She ran another glassful, looking out into the backyard. The elm tree's branches were obscured by its crop of new leaves, making it hard to see into the next yard. It seemed ridiculous to be dying in the spring. Jan gulped the second glass of water. It didn't help. *Fear has a taste,* she realized. Well, she wouldn't be tasting it for very much longer.

Back in the garage, Jan took a deep breath to steady herself, then started to run the duct tape around the seams of the door into the kitchen. It was a smaller door and didn't take as long. Once she was satisfied with the seal, she went over to her car and opened the door.

She slid behind the wheel, then leaned her head back against the headrest. This was it. She glanced at the clock on the dashboard and was amazed to see that less than an hour had passed since Aunt Leah had left. It seemed like much longer.

She leaned forward and put the key in the ignition. The soft chime warning of an open door began to ping. She stepped on the gas and started the car. The engine noise was louder than usual in the enclosed space, but it wasn't enough to drown out the door chime, which continued at one-second intervals. Such a tiny irritant shouldn't have made any difference under the circumstances, but it did. After a minute or so, Jan reached over and shut the door. The alarm stopped at once, and she sighed in relief. *That thing would have driven me crazy before I could kill myself.* She was shocked by her own morbid humor. She rolled down the car window. She wanted to get the full effects of the exhaust, to make this as fast as possible. Already the air stank from the fumes. Jan hadn't thought about how much she hated the smell of exhaust.

She leaned back again against the headrest, waiting for the carbon monoxide to overpower her and slide her painlessly out of life. Painless. She coughed once as the fumes caught at her throat, then continued as a choking spasm gripped her. Pain lanced through her newly healed throat as the coughs continued. The fit passed, leaving her panting. She gasped for breath, but by now the air was so heavy with exhaust, it didn't satisfy her lungs. Her stomach heaved at the taste of partially burnt gasoline on her tongue, and the lack of oxygen had her head pounding viciously. This wasn't painless. Jan's eyes were streaming, but she blinked the tears away enough to see the clock. Fifteen minutes had passed. This wasn't the way she'd thought it would be, but it wouldn't take much longer. It couldn't. . . .

All at once Jan didn't want to die anymore, she wanted to live. She fumbled for the door handle. It took several tugs before she could get it to open, then she almost fell, sliding out of the car. She pulled herself up against the open door. As soon as she was on her feet, a fresh fit of coughing seized her, doubling her over and almost making her fall again. Her throat felt as though it were on fire, from the combination of raw gasoline fumes and coughing. As soon as the door opened, the maddening little ping of the door chime had started again. She could stop it by reaching in to turn off the engine and take the keys out of the ignition, but she didn't have the strength. She had to get to the door to the house.

The door. It was only about ten feet away, but it seemed much farther. Her eyes were streaming constantly now, and she realized it wasn't just the fumes. She was crying for herself. This was stupid; she wasn't ready to die. But she was dying; she'd be dead soon if she couldn't get out of the garage. Her lungs heaved as she tried to pull air into them and felt the foul taste of exhaust in her mouth. She stumbled, at last reaching the steps to the side door. She tripped on the bottom step. Not bothering to try to regain her feet, she crawled up the two steps on her knees. The doorknob was out of reach; she had to stretch herself up against the door. She got her hand on the knob, and after the second try, she turned it. The door wouldn't open. The duct tape had sealed it shut.

She was coughing continuously now. Holding on to the knob, Jan dragged herself to her feet. Behind her the roar of the car's engine seemed to have grown louder, and the door chime clanged like a tolling bell. *They toll bells for dead people.*

With a last effort, Jan twisted the knob and fell against the door with her full weight. The tape gave way, and Jan collapsed onto the floor of the kitchen, her legs still in the garage.

TEN

Jan struggled up to her knees and, after a few wheezing breaths, staggered to the sink. She leaned over and opened the window all the way. Clean air. She gulped it down like water, savoring its purity. Then she opened the back door. Her head was pounding so hard, she whimpered in pain. But it was over. The madness was behind her now.

Wisps of foul-smelling exhaust were making their way into the kitchen from the open door, polluting the fresh air. Jan held her breath and plunged back into the haze-filled garage. She reached into the car and turned off the key, silencing the door alarm. The abrupt stillness was a relief. She spotted the clock; only seven minutes had passed since the last time she'd looked at it, the longest seven minutes of her life. Dropping the keys onto the front seat, she ran back to the kitchen for several more gulps of breathable air, then made her way back to the garage. She ripped the duct tape around the big door off and dropped it to the floor.

Once the door was open, the fresh spring breeze quickly dispersed the remaining fumes. Jan left the doors and windows of the house open as well, letting the last trace of exhaust blow away. While it did, she gathered the wadded-up lumps of silver tape and rags, hoping to remove all traces of what had happened in the garage that day.

Getting back into her car to pull out of the garage was rough. It would be a while before Jan could drive without remembering the terror she'd felt when she'd tried to escape the car earlier. She almost hadn't made it. Once the car was parked in its original spot, Jan returned to the house. By this time the headache was so bad, she had to squint to see past the pain. She got the various windows and doors shut, then went upstairs to her room and took a shower to wash off the stink of exhaust fumes. Finally, she fell into bed and into a deep, natural sleep.

* * *

Jan woke up when her aunt arrived home from the painting expedition. "Janelle?" she heard Aunt Leah call. "Dear, are you home?" Wincing, Jan sat up. The nap had taken away the sharpest edge of the headache, but a dull ache remained.

"I'm up here, Aunt Leah," she answered. She got to her feet. As she stood up, the pain flared briefly, then dropped to a steady throb. "I was taking a nap."

"I thought you'd gone out, I've been calling for several minutes," Aunt Leah said, poking her head in. "Sorry I woke you up." Her sharp eyes darted around the room, looking for evidence of trouble.

Jan forced a smile, hoping it didn't look as artificial as it felt. "I had a little headache; the nap helped."

"Well, come down when you feel like it."

Aunt Leah left, and Jan fell back onto the bed. She was calm now. When Jan had been in grade school, she'd had a very bad case of the flu. Her parents had worried as the fever soared to dangerous levels. It broke in a flood of sweat that soaked the sheets. Afterward Jan had felt weak, but she'd known she was okay. The rest

151

she'd had was restorative. She felt the same way now. She wouldn't try to kill herself again.

Her faith in her own innocence had returned. Something was going on, that was certain. Mr. Kahn was dead. Someone had set fire to the school. And she still had that foggy memory of swallowing endless pills. But now she was sure it hadn't been a real suicide attempt. The gaps in her memory bothered her, but she no longer thought they hid a murder.

Murder. That's what it was. Not only Mr. Kahn, but Jan herself. If she hadn't tried to commit suicide, someone had tried to kill her. She remembered swallowing the pills, but she shook the memory off. Some piece of that memory was missing.

Jan got up and prowled restlessly over to the window. She stared down at the street, not really seeing what she looked at. Sleepwalking. That's where it all started. What if she'd walked into a dangerous situation in her sleep? Like witnessing arson or murder?

But if she'd been sleepwalking when she witnessed someone setting a fire, and had been awake enough to know what was going on, why couldn't she remember anything? She was afraid it was tied to the holes in her memory. If someone she loved had been doing it, maybe her mind had suppressed it as too painful. Which would mean that someone she knew well was a murderer.

Jan knew from mystery novels that a good detective always looked for motive, method, and opportunity. The method was easy: so far, all the fires had been started with gasoline. That didn't take too much work, and it certainly didn't narrow the field of suspects any. Opportunity was just as wide open, at least on the fires. The phony files on her computer were tougher, and they *had* to be fakes. Several people had been in her room—family, kids from school. Most of them were competent with computers. According to the time stamps, the files had been written in the middle of the night, but there were programs that let you change time stamps. Mike had one, for instance. And of course, her family was right there, with access to her computer all the time.

The only motive that made any sense, at least for trying to drive Jan crazy, was fear. If she'd seen someone she knew committing a crime, and that person had seen her as well, the threat of arrest might have been enough. It was a one-size-fits-all motive; anyone could be guilty. That wouldn't explain the fires, though. Perhaps that was the *real* insanity in all this: pyromania.

Her mind veered back to the one thing she was sure of in this tangle of facts and suppositions. For the most part, everyone had had the opportunity to start fires. But the fire at the school was a little different. According to the investigator from the State Fire Marshal's Office, the journalism classroom hadn't been broken into. Someone had used a key.

And Mike was the only person besides Mr. Buehler who had a set of keys.

Suppertime came, and Jan went downstairs to join the family. The combination of churning emotions and the churning stomach left by the carbon monoxide had destroyed her appetite once again. Her raw throat hurt too badly to swallow anyway. She did manage to eat enough to deflect Aunt Leah's fussiness. She was congratulating herself on how well she'd concealed the suicide attempt, when Uncle Peter spoke and shook her confidence in the cleanup.

"Who left the garage door open?" he asked. "I've got a lot of expensive tools out there. The whole world could have walked right in."

Aunt Leah raised her eyebrows. Patting her

lips with her napkin, she said, "I parked out in front, my usual spot. I didn't even notice it was open." She looked at Jan.

Uncle Peter turned to glare at Jan as well. She must have forgotten to shut the garage door when she closed the others. Considering how much her head had been hurting, it was a wonder she'd managed to do any cleaning up at all.

"I'm sorry, Uncle Peter," Jan said. Her voice sounded normal, and she went on, encouraged by its steadiness. "I was going to go for a drive, but I noticed one of my tires was low. I drove in and used the compressor to fill it up, then I decided my head hurt too much to be driving. I guess I forgot."

"You didn't tell me you'd gone out," Aunt Leah said with a touch of sharpness.

"Well, I didn't," Jan muttered. After a couple more bites, she excused herself. She could feel her aunt watching as she left the room.

She went into the family room and looked at the phone for a moment. Then she picked it up. She called Julie first. Her friend sounded reluctant to talk with her, but Jan managed to keep her on the phone. Jan asked how the *Cat Claws* had been doing since the fire. Julie sounded suspicious, but she answered the question. The first postfire issue was almost ready, she told Jan.

Gradually Jan worked around to what she was *really* interested in. It was awkward, both because it was still hard to think about Mr. Kahn and because their fight had been the last time Julie had seen the counselor. But Jan had remembered something else that had happened that day. There'd been a substitute teacher, and he hadn't let them use the news office at lunchtime. Jan wondered why Mike hadn't let them in with his own keys. It was a puzzling point, but she didn't want to ask him about it. Yet.

Jan started discussing the editorial, which still choked her up. Soon Julie was crying as they talked about the counselor. Finally Jan said, "At least I got to see him one last time." Her own voice was thick with tears. "He had some bad news for me, but I don't care what the secretary says, I wasn't mad at him. Are you glad you got to see him that day?"

"I don't know," Julie said. "In a way I am, I guess, but he looked so *normal.* . . ."

There wasn't any reason for him not to look normal, Jan thought. *He didn't have a fatal disease!* But a lot of people said things like that when something tragic happened. "You know, we wouldn't have even been sent to see him and the principal if that sub had let us eat in the classroom. You got there before I did; how come Mike didn't just use his keys?" She held her breath, waiting for the answer.

"He said he'd lost them," Julie told her. "So we wound up in the lunchroom, and we had that fight, and we had to see Mr. Kahn. . . ." When Julie spoke again, there was suspicion in her voice. "How come you're asking about Mr. Kahn all of a sudden, anyway?"

"Mike came over last night and typed up the editorial on my computer," Jan said. It was an honest answer, even if it wasn't a complete one. "I read it. It got me thinking."

"It was good, wasn't it?" Julie paused for so long, Jan thought she'd hung up. "I think it will help a lot of kids."

They said good-bye a few minutes later, and Jan dialed Barb's number. She hadn't seen the photographer since she'd been in the hospital. Although Barb hadn't been there during the fight, Jan managed to get another confirmation of her suspicion. Mike no longer seemed to have his keys, and he hadn't since the day before the fire in the school.

Jan didn't know if Mike was involved or not.

He might have hidden the keys, to deflect suspicion after the fire. Or they could be genuinely lost, for anyone to find and use. No doubt there were several other sets of keys floating around. The janitors surely had keys, and the principal probably had a set too.

Aunt Leah came into the family room while Jan sat there thinking. "How's your headache now, Janelle?"

"Oh, sorry," Jan said, snapping out of it. "I didn't see you. It's gotten worse. Do you think Dr. Holsinger would let me have some aspirin?"

"I have something much better," her aunt replied. "And you don't need a doctor's approval for it." *Oh, no,* Jan thought. Aunt Leah left the room and returned a few minutes later with a steaming mug of her favorite cure-all tea. "Drink this, and then maybe you should go back to bed."

Well, she'd brought it on herself, and the stuff really did help sometimes. This time Jan managed to drink the whole bitter mugful. Then she said good night and went up to bed. Her head was pounding again, whether from the lingering effects of the morning or from wondering about Mike, Jan couldn't say. Before she got ready for bed, she rummaged through the bathroom medicine cabinet, but there wasn't so much as a cough drop. Dr. Holsinger had been emphatic that Jan avoid all medicine for a while, and she'd refused to refill the prescription for the sleepwalking remedy. Jan wondered what the doctor would have thought about carbon monoxide as a cure for headaches.

As she lay in bed, trying to find a comfortable position on a pillow that seemed to be stuffed with bricks, Jan thought again about the first "suicide" attempt. That was really the part that made no sense. Fires were easy to start, but how could you make someone kill herself? This morning's failed attempt proved that Jan didn't want to die. But she could still see herself holding those pills, taking the glass of water, swallowing them. . . .

Taking the glass! She sat up abruptly, headache forgotten. She reached for the memory. Yes, she'd been sitting here in bed, tablets in her hand. And someone had handed her a glass of water. *Someone.* Jan couldn't find a face to go with the memory, she didn't even see a hand. But she hadn't had the water until someone gave it to her. Someone who had probably also given her the tablets. And Jan had swallowed them, and swallowed some more, and more, without knowing what she was doing.

That someone had tried to kill her and had almost succeeded. As Jan settled back down, she realized something else. Whoever it was would probably try again.

She was sleeping, in her old bed, in her old house. But the soft voice was insistent. "Jan, wake up. You have to wake up, honey. Get up, Jan. . . ."

She didn't want to get up. It wasn't morning yet. But her mother was calling her, her voice more demanding than ever. "Jan, right now. You have to get out of bed. Hurry, before it's too late. Hurry. . . ." The dream voice of her mother faded as Jan swung her feet out of bed and got up. It was autumn and the room was cold. She pulled her robe tightly around herself as she approached the door. Something was waiting on the other side of the door. She opened it, and the lace ruffles on her sleeve caught fire like a torch, and she was burning, burning. . . .

The room blurred and shifted around her. Jan looked down at the plain sleeve of her nightgown. This was her room now, her new room, and the air was chill but carried the breath of spring. But she could still hear her mother's voice. There was a note of desperate urgency in the soundless whisper now.

"Jan, you must wake up. Wake up! Be careful. . . ."

Jan opened her eyes. She felt heavy, tired; all she wanted to do was go back to sleep. But Mom said she had to get up. Mom was calling. . . .

She wasn't in bed. For a moment Jan thought she was trapped in another nightmare, this one a repeat of the fire at the Blue Willow. But the building burning in front of her wasn't a restaurant. It was Julie's house, and Jan was so close to the flames, she could feel the heat in her mouth, her nose, her eyes.

She tried to step back, and for the first time realized that someone was holding her arms, forcing her toward the fire. Jan struggled, but her muscles weren't responding. She tried to turn her head to see who was holding her, but one of the cruel hands released an arm and grabbed her hair, pulling it so hard, Jan cried out from the sharp pain. The other hand still held her right arm in a steel grip.

Abruptly her arm and hair were released, so

suddenly she almost stumbled. Before Jan could turn, she felt a blow on the back of her head. Her knees started to crumple under her, but the hands were back, holding her up for a moment.

Then a voice, distorted beyond recognition, said, "Now, *die!*" as Jan felt the hands shove her into the flames.

ELEVEN

Jan fell forward through the open doorway, landing hard on her knees inside the fire-filled kitchen of the Rodgerses' house. For a moment she knelt there, her head pounding from the blow. Then she reached around and felt the back of her head gingerly. There was a wetness she was sure could only be blood.

An intense flare of heat washed over her as a ceiling panel sagged near her, melting plastic dripping in long globs that burst into flame as they fell. She had to get out. An acrid odor of burning hair was added to all the other smells, and she knew her own curls were smoldering. Jan started to get to her feet, then stopped. The door was still open behind her. The fresh air fed the blaze, but it also meant the air near the floor would stay breathable. She started crawling backward, feeling behind her with her bare feet as she inched toward the open door and safety.

The metal strip across the threshold burned her toes as she stubbed against it. She hurriedly backed the rest of the way out, skinning her knees and ripping her thin nightgown on the rough brick sidewalk. As soon as she was outside, she scrambled to her feet and ran. There was no sign of whoever had pushed her into the fire; maybe her assailant had left, assuming Jan was unconscious from the blow.

There were no sirens, no activity in the neighborhood beyond the growing noise of the fire itself. Julie! She and her family must still be asleep.

Her nightgown was streaked with soot and blood at the knees. If she was spotted, no one would ever believe that she hadn't set the fire. But she couldn't let the Rodgerses die. She looked around, frantic, searching for a way to rouse them. Near the garden shed was a small pile of bricks. Jan ran for it, not even noticing the sharp stones and twigs under her feet. Grabbing a couple of bricks, she ran to the back of the house. The double windows above her were in Julie's parents' room. Jan threw the first brick through the left-hand window as hard as she could.

The crash of shattering glass was echoed by a lesser crash, as the brick knocked down the venetian blinds inside the window. Within seconds a light went on in the room, and Jan heard a cry. They must have smelled the smoke.

Whirling, she ran toward the nearest house with the other brick. Someone needed to phone the fire department. She selected what looked like a bedroom window and pitched the remaining brick. The reaction wasn't quite as dramatic, but a light came on, and Jan saw someone come to the window. From where the figure was, the fire at the Rodgerses' was easily visible.

Jan stuck around for a while, wanting to make sure help was on the way. She was well hidden in the bushes, but suppressing her coughs had become almost impossible. The combination of smoke inhalation and her still-tender throat was ripping her in two as she fought to control the urge. Within minutes she heard sirens approaching. Julie's parents stumbled out of the front door, coughing, but Julie herself was nowhere in sight. Moments later, when the first fire truck arrived, the fire fighters spoke briefly with the Rodgerses; then some of them ran for a ladder. Propping it against the side of the house, one started climbing. Jan watched, her heart pounding with fear; that was Julie's room. He knocked out the glass and climbed through the window. Below, a medic was trying to give oxygen to Julie's parents. Both of them ignored the masks, staring instead at their daughter's window. In less than a minute, the fire fighter climbed back out, Julie draped over his shoulder. From the way her arms dangled, it was obvious that she was unconscious, but she was out of the burning house. Flames were visible now through the broken bedroom window.

An ambulance had arrived, and Julie was quickly loaded into it, Mrs. Rodgers climbing in after her. The ambulance drove off at high speed, blue lights flashing, the two-toned siren adding another note of confusion to the night. After it left, Julie's dad stood talking excitedly to a man who had emerged from an unmarked car, obviously describing the crashing brick that had awakened them and saved their lives. From this distance Jan couldn't be sure, but she thought it was Mr. Randall, the fire inspector. It was time to go.

Jan didn't feel strong enough to make it back

to her aunt and uncle's place. The adrenaline that had gotten her this far had worn off, and she had a double headache, from the smoke and the blow. She reached back and felt the tender area, wincing as her fingers encountered an oozing patch. It had been a hard blow, and the scalp was torn. Her skull didn't seem to be cracked, but waves of agony radiated from the wound. Blurring the edge of exhaustion and adrenaline letdown was a dull, fuzzy feeling, as though she'd been drugged again. *Maybe I was drugged,* she thought. It would explain how she'd been transported almost a mile without waking up. The arsonist had to have brought her here and then set the fire. And Jan had slept through most of it. If she hadn't had that dream about her mother calling her . . .

She wasn't sure it had been a dream, but she'd worry about that later. Right now she needed to get home, and she was going to need help. She was shaking violently. Spring or not, it was too chilly to be wandering around in bare feet and a tattered nightgown.

Jan moved through the bushes, sticking to backyards as much as she could. Despite her best efforts, her progress wasn't soundless; if anyone had been there, they could have heard rustles in the bushes and soft cries as thorns raked her legs and arms. But no one was around to hear. Staying out of sight was the crucial thing now.

Jan paused to rest for a moment. She could still hear the noises of the fire fighters, a block away, and the flashing lights from the fire trucks cast crazy shadows through the branches. By now Jan was panting and shaking so hard, she knew she couldn't make it home unassisted. There was one place she could turn to for help, and it scared her. Mike lived near here.

If her worst suspicions were true—if Mike was the one behind this—then turning to him for help was the stupidest thing she'd ever do. And it could well be the *last* thing she'd do. In her mind she heard that voice once again, the distorted snarl saying *"Die!"* She couldn't identify it, but it hadn't sounded like Mike. And the hands on her arms hadn't felt like Mike's hands. She knew their touch.

I can't be sure, she thought grimly, *but I don't have much choice. And if it* was *Mike* . . .

Like many of the older homes in Kenowa, Mike's house was raised above a basement, with steps leading up to the porch. Fortunately, his room was on the ground floor. Standing on her tiptoes she could barely reach the bottom of the window. She tapped on the wooden frame for what seemed like hours before Mike's face appeared above her.

He was bare-chested, staring out into the yard with a puzzled expression. She rapped once more, and he lowered his gaze. Spotting her, he dropped to his knees and raised the window a crack.

"Jan!" It was a fierce whisper. "What the hell are you doing?" His eyes took in the nightgown and blood, and he added, "What happened? Are you all right?"

Jan slumped against the side of the house, all the strength suddenly gone from her body. She said nothing, concentrating instead on keeping on her feet.

"Jan?" The whisper was more urgent, but she still couldn't manage to say anything. Mike seemed to understand this; he said, "Okay, hang on a minute," then vanished from sight. She leaned against the siding, holding desperately on to the wood. At the moment, she didn't think she'd be able to move if the entire fire department drove into the yard and shone spotlights on her.

There was a squeal of wood, and the window above her head slid up the rest of the way. Mike threw his legs over the sill and dropped lightly down beside Jan. He'd thrown on a pair of jeans and a sweatshirt, and he had an extra one in his hands for Jan. She struggled into it, grateful for the warmth, then followed him quietly around the side of the house. His car was parked in the alley behind the house, and they slid into the front seat. Once they were there, he put his arm around her and pulled her close.

"All right, Jan, we can talk now," he said. His voice was still low. "What's going on? You look like hell, and you've got scratches all over you, and blood, and . . ." He stopped and sniffed. "Smoke. Has there been another fire?" He hesitated, then finished, "Did you start it?"

Jan leaned against his chest, savoring the warmth and firmness of his arm. Without moving, she said, "I didn't start it, no. It was Julie's place. But I woke up there, and someone *pushed* me into the fire. Mike, it wasn't just a dream this time, there was someone there."

She felt his arm tighten slightly. Gently he asked, "Who was it? Did you get a look at them?"

As gentle as his voice was, she could hear

disbelief in every syllable. She pulled away from him, sitting up within the circle of his arm. "No. Whoever it was grabbed me and wouldn't let me look around. But it was real, and this time I've got some proof." She took his fingers and guided them to the back of her skull, her breath hissing slightly as his fingers found the spot. "They tried to knock me out before pushing me into the fire, only it didn't work." As his fingers probed, she winced again. "Careful, that hurts."

"No joke," he said. His voice was grim. "Contrary to what you see on TV, it isn't all that easy to knock a person out. You might have a concussion. That's a nasty crack. How long ago did all this happen?" As he spoke, another siren wailed past on the streets. "Couldn't have been that long ago, from the feel—the blood's still sticky."

"It feels like it's been a year, but I guess maybe a half hour or forty-five minutes." She felt the wound. It was oozing slightly, but didn't seem too bad. Just painful. "Not more than an hour, and I don't think it was that long. The longest part was waiting for the fire trucks. I threw a brick through a window to wake up the Rodgerses."

171

She could see the gleam of his teeth as he grinned. "That sounds logical. So what do we do now? I take it you don't want to go watch the fire. . . ."

"Hardly." She shivered. "The family's out, I stayed long enough to see that. They took Julie away in an ambulance, but I think she's alive. But . . ."

He waited as she thought, biting her lip. She felt safe now, convinced Mike had nothing to do with the fires and murder attempts. But *some-one* had pushed her toward that door into an inferno. She didn't want to chance it happening again. And she'd been asleep, supposedly "safe" in her own bed.

Slowly, thinking things out a word at a time, Jan said, "I still don't know who's doing all of this. Or why. I've got to figure that out before someone else gets hurt. What time is it?"

He pushed the button on the side of his watch, lighting the display. Her eyes focused on the digits. It was later than she'd realized, almost five A.M. The eastern sky was still dark, but before long it would start to lighten. Jan yawned suddenly, as a new wave of fatigue hit her. She shook her head, as much to throw off sleep as anything else. "In a way, it's a good

172

thing it's so late. I have to get back before everyone wakes up, but I don't want to go to sleep until I figure out what's going on." Unconsciously her fingers strayed to the back of her head as she added, "It might not be safe."

"I'm not so sure you *should* go home," Mike said, his lips brushing her hair. "Someone got you out of there before, and I'll bet the cops will be asking you questions come daylight."

"Yeah," Jan agreed. "That's going to be a problem." She slumped against him. "I don't know how I'll convince them I didn't do anything. I mean, they have me down as a nut case anyway, with that so-called suicide and everything. . . ."

He interrupted her. "You didn't try to kill yourself?" he demanded. There were tears in his eyes as he held her tightly.

"No," she said simply. "I'm not suicidal. But the cops think I am."

"That tore me up, thinking you hurt so badly you'd kill yourself and you hadn't even told me —that hurt. And it scared me." She could feel his lips brushing her hair again.

"Take me home," she commanded, sitting up in sudden decision. "I'll take a shower and make sure someone sees me, so they won't think I was out all night. Then, when Andrea leaves for school and Uncle Peter goes to work, I'll duck out before the cops can get there and spend the day hiding. . . ."

"Where?" he asked. It was a good question, and she didn't have an answer.

"I don't know," she admitted. "Someplace where I can take a nap and figure out what to do."

"I'll pick you up," Mike said, starting the car. "And I'm going to sit outside the house till you come out. My mom's heading to St. Louis in the morning, and Arnie's on the road. I'll ditch school."

Her protests died on her lips. Maybe, with some help, she could finally discover who was behind it all.

Mike let the car coast to a halt three doors down from the Scotts' house. He'd driven on side streets, avoiding the official vehicles still clustered around Julie's house. Jan half ran, half stumbled across the front lawn, hoping the front door would be unlocked. She reached the house and climbed the stairs gingerly, trying to avoid the board that creaked. Once she got her hand on the knob and eased it open, she let out the breath she'd been holding. It was open. She looked back over her shoulder to Mike's car, hidden in the dark under the Simpsons' elm trees. It wasn't visible, but Jan felt protected, just knowing Mike was there. She slipped inside and closed the door gently behind her.

Once upstairs, she stopped worrying about keeping quiet as she went to take a shower. She had to get the smell of smoke washed off, and she was *supposed* to be in her room. She was almost afraid to touch the bump on her head, which by now was swollen to the size of a golf ball. The multitude of scratches she'd picked up in the bushes all stung like paper cuts, but she ignored them as best she could. She hurried to put on another nightgown, a clean one, and stuffed the filthy and tattered thing she'd taken off into her gym bag. Once it was zipped and hidden at the back of her closet shelf, she relaxed somewhat. She'd get rid of it during the day. For the moment there was nothing obvious to connect her to the fire at the Rodgerses'.

She sat up by the window, fighting to keep herself awake as dawn intensified. Mike's car, deep in the shadows, was still almost invisible, but she knew he was awake. As soon as she'd felt his hands on her arms, she'd been sure he wasn't the one who had held her so cruelly. Only one doubt nagged at her now—the question about his keys.

At last she heard her uncle stirring downstairs. This was her best chance. Aunt Leah asked too many questions. Jan got dressed, then grabbed her purse and backpack. The gym bag with her nightgown was tucked into her backpack, buried beneath several books. She went down the stairs, careful to make more noise than normal, and breezed into the kitchen. If she could carry the act off for five minutes, she'd be home free.

"Hi, Uncle Peter," she greeted him. He straightened up, looking startled.

"Jan! This is a surprise, I don't think I've seen you up this early in a month." He looked wary. "I take it you're feeling a little better?"

"Lots better," she said, hoping that the shower and her grin were enough to disguise the fatigue weighing her down. "In fact, I want to get out for a while. I've been inside too much lately."

"Janny, I'm not so sure that's a good idea," he said seriously. "The doctor said you didn't have to go back to school yet."

Shouldn't go back, you mean. Jan had heard

that comment from Dr. Holsinger, right before she'd left the hospital. It had been only a few days ago, but it felt like ancient history. *That was a different Jan,* she thought, *one who believed she was guilty. I know better now.*

"I'm not going to school, don't worry," she promised. "I just thought I'd go for a drive, maybe stop and take a walk . . ." As she spoke, she rummaged in the refrigerator for some food. She tucked a couple of apples into the side of her backpack, then grabbed half a bag of rice cakes. "Have sort of a picnic," she finished, zipping her bag closed over the food. "I don't know how far I'll go, maybe all the way to St. Louis. I'll call if it gets too late." Jan could hear her aunt coming down the stairs now. She grabbed a slice of toast out of her uncle's hand and headed for the door, saying, "Thanks, Uncle Peter, later, bye!" She let the screen door bang closed behind her and ran out to her car.

Once there, she threw her stuff in the back and started it with a roar. She watched the rearview mirror, hoping Mike would follow her lead. He did, pulling in behind her as she turned onto Main Street. She led the way to the edge of town and onto a series of county roads.

Once they were well into farmland, she pulled off the road and stopped.

He stopped behind her. Coming up to the open window, he asked, "What's the deal? I thought you were coming with me."

Jan shook her head. "It's better this way. If they thought I was on foot, they'd figure I was someplace close. Now I could be anywhere, and they'll be looking for the car. *If* they look, that is. They may not, but I have a hunch they will. Now we just have to figure out someplace to hide the car for the day."

"There's an old grain elevator down about a mile that way," he said, pointing. "No one ever goes there. C'mon, I'll lead."

She followed him to the derelict structure and parked close to its base, then climbed in beside him. As she did, he glanced at his watch. "I think there's still time," he muttered. "You aren't the only one who's been doing some thinking. I'm going to school, at least for a few classes. See what everyone's saying, fix up an alibi, you know. I'll drop you off at the house, and you can grab some sleep while I play innocent." He grinned at her. "Jan? Jan who?"

* * *

When Jan stretched out on the bed in Mike's room, she immediately fell asleep. At first it was dreamless, as though she'd exhausted her capacity for dreaming. Then, gradually, it shifted into the familiar dreamscape, but this time with a difference. This time Jan knew she was dreaming. It was more like watching a movie than living through it once more. . . .

Jan could see herself lying in bed. Beyond the door, she knew, flames were consuming the house. Her parents were in their bed, past knowledge, past help. But still, she could hear her mother's insistent call to wake up, get up.

The figure on the bed stirred, responding to the call. The smoke detector in the hall was silent, although the fumes were already noticeable in the room. Jan watched herself get up and wrap the robe around herself, then approach the door. She opened the door, and the flames engulfed her arm. This time Jan didn't feel the pain.

Her dream-self was dragging the quilt off the bed, wrapping it around the blazing sleeve, then stumbling over to the window. The room was on the second floor. As Jan watched, her image opened the window, sat on the sill, then pushed herself away from the building as she fell. Jan watched herself land in a rolling dive. Her face was distorted with pain from her arm and with grief as she looked up at the house, now fully engulfed.

"Mom! Dad!" She was screaming their names repeatedly, as the tears streamed down her face. "Mom!" Jan watched herself in horror, feeling real tears wet on her own cheeks even through the dream. At last the fire trucks arrived, and the ambulance with the paramedics. As they started to treat her, asking questions, Jan could feel the memory of horror sliding away, hiding behind a veil of oblivion from a mind too hurt to bear it. It would be months before that veil was torn.

"Mom. Dad!" Jan sat up abruptly. Mike was there, holding her as the memories forced their way out in a flood of tears. For all the pain, there was a deep comfort in knowing, at last, that she wasn't responsible for her parents' death. "I didn't kill them, Mike. I didn't."

She clung to him sobbing for an unmeasured time. Gradually she regained control of herself. The fall of light in the room had shifted; several hours had passed. She sat back. His face was grave as he held her. She smiled at him. Her eyes were puffy from crying, but it was the happiest smile she'd felt in ages. "I didn't hurt them," she whispered.

TWELVE

"What was school like?" Jan asked after her tears had subsided. She sat back, running a hand through her hair.

"Everyone was talking," he said. The worried expression on his face pushed the remnants of her dream to the back of her mind. *But I didn't do it.* The thought lingered as she focused on what Mike was saying. "Julie's house was almost destroyed. She's in the hospital. Barb said she'll make it, but she was burned pretty badly. And everyone knows Julie was the one who told the cops about your sleepwalking. It's all over school, along with the rumor you had a fight with her the other day about telling them." He stopped, as though debating the next part, then went on. "That's just rumors, there've been a lot of those lately. But Barb talked to me after English. That's why I cut out earlier than I planned."

Jan twisted around to see the clock. It was only eleven, well before lunch hour.

"Remember when she saw you at the Foote place, after the fire there? She didn't think anything about it at the time, but she told me about it, and it bothered me. I didn't know why. And she took a couple of pictures of you. She showed them to me when you were in the hospital after the suicide attempt. . . ." He broke off as she shook her head. "Sorry, after the murder attempt. They got me even more upset."

Mike pulled an envelope out of his pocket and withdrew several photos. He gave two of them to Jan. She could see why they had disturbed him. They were stark photos of ruin, and Jan was shown staring at the destruction with a strange expression.

"I don't think she ever realized what they might mean," Mike went on. "You know Barb lives only a few houses down from Julie. She got some pictures of the fire last night. She was planning on selling them to the *Chronicle*, but then she developed them during first hour and . . ." Wordlessly he handed the remaining photos to her. They were dramatic shots of a fire at night, showing flames shooting from the roof, paramedics, an ambulance, fire fighters with grim faces. The black-and-white photos had drama and impact. Jan didn't see anything in them beyond that. She looked at him, her face full of questions.

"You don't see it?" He took the last picture and held it up. It was a full view of the scene, with fire fighters pouring water onto the side of the blazing house. Mutely he pointed to the background. There, almost obscured by the trees and bushes behind the house, was a faint smudge of white. Jan didn't have to use a magnifying glass to realize it was a picture of her in her nightgown.

"I can't make out the face," she said.

"Neither can I, but I wouldn't count on that being any help. It's you, isn't it? The cops will be able to enlarge it. Besides, do you think anyone is going to need to see a face?" Mike took the pictures from her numbed fingers and slipped them back into the envelope. "Barb didn't. She showed it to me and said she hadn't believed the rumors until now. It's either someone in a nightgown, or a ghost, and by now

184

everyone in town knows who goes wandering around all the time at two A.M. in her nightie."

There wasn't an answer to that. Instead Jan asked, "How'd you get the pictures?"

"I asked Barb to let me have them. I told her I was going to try to find you, convince you to go to the police," he said. "I figure we've maybe got the rest of today and tonight. By tomorrow she'll call the cops, and I'll be answering questions as well." He dropped down beside her on the bed. "We'd better come up with some answers, or they're likely to lock us *both* up."

"Mike, where are your keys to the newspaper office?" Jan asked, wanting to clear the air. "Julie told me you'd lost them. The firebug used a key to get into the journalism room."

"Yeah, I know." He paused, uncomfortable, then blurted it out. "That was when I started thinking maybe you weren't crazy, maybe you were doing it on purpose. The night before you came back to school, after the plastic surgery— I was over that night, remember? I got home and I couldn't find my keys. I almost pulled the seat out of the car looking for them, but they were gone. So I figured I'd dropped them at your place. I thought you'd mention them the next day, but instead . . ." His face was grim.

185

"Instead, you had that fight with Julie. And that night someone used a key to get into the classroom."

"And you thought I'd taken them," she whispered. It was a wonder he hadn't gone to the police himself, a long time ago. She said so, finishing with the question, "Why didn't you?"

With one finger he lifted her chin and looked her square in the eyes. "I asked myself that about a million times. I guess, deep down, I just couldn't believe you'd kill someone." He leaned forward and kissed her gently, a kiss that grew in intensity. *He believed in me,* Jan thought, as she pulled herself closer to him. The knowledge was even warmer than the kiss.

After a while Mike drew back and said, "So neither one of us had the keys. There's one thing I don't understand, though. Why did you suspect *me*? I mean, I could have set the fires, I guess, but what reason would I have? And there's no way I could have followed you around while you were sleepwalking. Or last night—do you think I could have gotten into your house and dragged you out without waking everyone up?"

"I was afraid it *had* to be you because I love

you. I know it doesn't make much sense." That caused another short interruption, as Mike kissed her again.

"You're right, that doesn't make sense," he said softly, touching her cheek gently.

"There are too many things I don't remember," Jan said in a flat voice. She stared in front of her as she ran the memories of the last six weeks through her mind. "I've done some sleepwalking, but there are things I *know* I'm forgetting! I didn't remember Andrea telling me about the concert. I don't know how all that stuff got on my computer. Books out of place. Things like that. And . . ." She swallowed hard, keeping her voice steady with an effort. "And there was someone else in the room during that 'suicide' attempt. Someone gave me all those pills to take, and I can't remember who. I thought maybe I didn't *want* to remember who it was. If it was you—if you were trying to hurt me, I might not have wanted to know about it."

She tried to lick her lips, but her mouth had suddenly gone dry. "I didn't remember there was anyone with me until after I really tried to kill myself."

She'd gotten it out. There was silence for a moment, then Mike's hands grasped her arms and pulled her around to face him. She could feel the difference, now, between his gentle hands and the ones that had pushed her into the fire. "Jan. Tell me."

The entire story of the second, genuine suicide attempt came pouring out. Little more than twenty-four hours had passed, and so much else had happened during that time. Now the horror of it hit her hard. Mike's arms were around her, and she was in tears before she was halfway done. She went on to her sudden memory of the hand holding a glass of water for her and the dream that had awakened her outside of Julie's. When she finished, his arms tightened.

"Thank God," he said quietly. "Thank God you're all right."

"I really did think I was insane," Jan said.

"You weren't," he said. His voice was tight with rigidly controlled anger. "I think I know who's been doing this to you," he said, pulling her against him. "Can't you figure it out?"

She shook her head, wondering. Almost—*almost*—she could make out the shadowy figure holding the glass out, urging her to swallow. . . . It was no use. Her mind wouldn't take that final step.

"From what you've said, I think you've been drugged for a long time," he said bluntly. "If your mind's been wiped out by sleeping pills and barbs and God-knows-what, that would explain a lot of the sleepwalking and blanks. A lot, but not all. You thought it was me because I'm close to you. There's someone closer, at least physically." Protests rose to her lips, but died as he continued. "Your cousin. Andrea."

"Andrea?" As Jan said the name, more foggy memories arose in her mind. Andrea sitting at the computer, her reaction to Mr. Kahn's death, Andrea crying as she coaxed Jan to take another pill . . . "But why?" Jan asked the question wildly, her mind whirling. "We were never that close before—before the first fire, but I didn't think she hated me! She didn't, I *know* she didn't. And she was devastated by what happened to Mr. Kahn—I can't believe she did it herself!" But too many pieces of the puzzle were falling into place now. Even as Jan denied it, she found herself accepting the fact that Andrea was guilty.

"I doubt if she ever intended to hurt him," Mike said. His face reflected Jan's own pain. "Maybe at first she didn't even intend to hurt you physically, just drive you into a complete breakdown. But she's got a motive, a *real* motive, not just craziness." At Jan's blank look, he asked, "Who owns Scott and Company now?"

"Uncle Peter's running it, but I'm majority owner, since Daddy died. . . ." Her voice trailed off as she realized what that meant. Mike spelled it out anyway.

"Your dad started the company. Uncle Peter was always the junior partner. From what you've said, everything your parents owned came to you; Peter didn't get any more of the company. If you died now, everything would go to him and your aunt. And Andrea is an only child. Someday she'll be rich, if you're out of the way. And even if you aren't buddy-buddy, she's still your cousin. Family. It's no wonder your mind blanked out."

Jan knew that Aunt Leah had never really cared for her. It had never occurred to her, though, that Andrea might share her mother's feelings and resent Jan's inheritance. Resent it enough to commit murder.

"Mike, if you're right, how am I ever going to prove it?" Jan asked. "It would *really* sound crazy if I went to the cops with this story! The fire marshal thinks I'm the arsonist."

Mike stood up and started pacing. "Jan, I want you to try to remember everything that made you think you were crazy," he urged. "We can't find out anything about the fires that the state fire marshal doesn't already know, so let's focus on the attacks on you. The physical attacks, and the ones on your sanity." He stopped at his desk and grabbed a long yellow legal pad. "Maybe we can figure something out from them."

Her muddy slippers, the gas-soaked sleeve of her robe, open doors, shifted books, her near fall down the stairs—for the next hour Jan struggled to push the cobwebs aside and *remember* everything. Before they'd been at it very long, her head was aching, and the familiar blurry feeling was back. If Mike was right and she'd been drugged for weeks, she was probably addicted to whatever she'd been fed. Each time she'd seen the plastic surgeon, there'd been pain pills, more than she could use. There should have been some left, but there weren't. The same thing with the sleepwalking medicine she'd gotten from Dr. Holsinger. By themselves those pills probably weren't enough to account for all the fog. Still, they would have been a start. Jan had no idea how Andrea had done it, but she and Mike could figure that out later.

At last she ran down. Mike looked through his pages of notes. "There's nothing concrete here, but I'm convinced. Andrea's room connects to yours; it would be easy for her to pull all that on you. A lot of it is just misdirection. You don't remember her telling you about the concert because she didn't. And so on. As long as you figured she was telling the truth, it would look like *you* were the one with some loose connections. Once you turn it around, though . . ."

"Yeah," she said. "Only we still can't prove it."

"If there's proof, it'll be at your place," he said. "Is your aunt home right now?"

She looked at the clock. Almost one already. "She might be, but normally she's got her garden club meeting. What were you planning?"

He reached for the phone. "If she's not there, we might take a fast look around, see if we can find anything." He dialed, and the wait seemed endless as he let it ring. Finally he put it down and said, "I let it ring sixteen times. We'll give it a try. Let's hope she's not just out for a walk."

They drove over to her house, and Mike

192

parked openly in front. "We only have to hide you right now, not me," he told her. He knocked at the door, then used Jan's key to let himself in. After several minutes he came back out to the car.

"The coast is clear. If she comes in, you duck out the back way and I'll give her a song and dance about looking for you."

They went in together. "Keep an eye on the time," Jan warned him. "Andrea has student council after school, but she'll be home by four."

Jan started searching Andrea's room, while Mike went through the family room. Jan really didn't know what she was looking for, but something like an empty prescription bottle or gasoline-scented clothes would be good. All of Andrea's clutter was hidden in her dresser drawers and closets, which were a jumble. It made things easier, in a way; Jan didn't have to worry about messing things up. On the other hand, it slowed her down, since things like medicine bottles could be hidden in a tangle of clothes. But there was nothing.

At last, with a glance at the clock on Andrea's bed table, she gave up. It was almost two thirty, and she didn't want to risk being caught. Jan was halfway down the stairs when Mike started up them two at a time.

"Did you find something?" she asked eagerly.

"I think so," he said, heading back into the family room and across to the bookshelf. "See what you think of this."

Mike had several books pulled off the bottom shelf. Jan had never really looked through them; that section mainly held her uncle's old college texts. Mike handed one to her. It certainly looked like a textbook. She glanced at the book's spine and felt a chill go down her own. There were library call numbers glued to the base of the spine.

Jan opened the book. The little envelope inside the cover still held its card; the book hadn't been checked out. She read the title: *Souls in Torment—Poetry and Prose from the Dark Side of the Spirit.*

"Tell me if this sounds familiar," Mike said, flipping to a poem near the beginning. Jan started to read it, nearly dropping the book in amazement after the first few lines.

"This—Mike, it's the crazy stuff from my poem about spring!" She read down a few more lines. There was no question; almost word for word, it was the same distorted verse that had been grafted onto her own work. She turned back to the beginning and skimmed through the forward. The book was a compilation of essays and poetry by the severely mentally ill.

She flipped through it, phrases and sentences catching her eye as she did. All of the strange files on her computer seemed to have been copied from this book. She stopped. There was the "suicide" note, or most of it. It was an actual note, left by a schizophrenic who had killed herself. No wonder it had all sounded genuine. It was.

"That's not all," Mike said grimly. "Here, hold these. . . ." He handed her another two books, then pushed the rest together so the gap wasn't noticeable. "Let's get out of here and take the books with us."

They hurried back to the car, and Jan slouched down in the seat as they roared through the streets. School was out by now, and she didn't want to be seen. Once they reached Mike's place, he hustled her into the house after checking in all directions for observers.

Once they were inside, she sat down to examine the other books. The first was the one about sleepwalking she'd looked at in the library, the other a text on abnormal psychology. She leafed through it, pausing when she got to the chapter on multiple personalities. "I thought this was what was wrong with me," she said, showing him the chapter.

He shook his head. "Jan, that is so rare. . . . Look, if it'd been something like that, it would have turned up before your parents died." He took the book from her and closed it. "Spend too much time looking at that, you really will go crazy."

"You realize these aren't exactly proof, don't you?" she asked. "They were stolen from the library. As a matter of fact, I turned in a report. They might think I stole them myself."

"Doesn't matter," Mike said. "It doesn't take a shrink to figure out all the crap on your computer was copied from this. The whole thing's based on making it look like you were freaked out. If you were crazy, you wouldn't have been copying this."

"I guess so." Jan set the books down. "Only what do we do now?"

For the next hour Mike and Jan worked out a plan of attack. Mike's mom called around five thirty, to tell him she was spending the night in

St. Louis with the old roommate she'd gone to visit. Since his stepdad wasn't due back for another three days, that meant they had the house to themselves.

Mike didn't want to let Jan go home at all, but she insisted. "Mike, I have to face Andrea. I don't think she'll try anything in front of her parents, and I have to *know*, before I call the police. I owe Uncle Peter and Aunt Leah that much, anyway. It's going to be rough on them, finding out what she's done."

"Yeah, no joke," Mike said, shaking his head. "It's been a little rough on you, too, don't forget that. She's tried to kill you at least twice."

"I think," Jan spoke slowly, "that I'll take a nap now and have you take me home late. I'll confront her. And then . . ." She stopped, knowing he wasn't going to like this part.

"And then?" he prompted her.

"And then I'll pretend to go to bed. Only I won't go to sleep. You can park the car where you did last night and wait. If she knows I've figured it out, she may make one last try at killing me." *This is* really *insane*, Jan thought, *I'm talking about someone killing me like I was in a movie!* "Then we'll have her."

"Jan, have you gone nuts?" The furious ques-

197

tion brought Mike up short as soon as he said it. She couldn't help it; she burst out laughing. After a moment he began to laugh as well, but he stopped almost as quickly as he'd started. "All right, scratch that. We already proved you haven't. But painting a target on your back this way sure sounds a little crazy to me."

"I know," she said. "But it's fair, and it's what I'm going to do. We just have to be careful, that's all."

It was almost eleven when Jan let herself in.

"Jan!" Aunt Leah came out into the hall at the sound of the door and stopped in amazement. "Where have you been all day? Why didn't you call?"

"I've just been around," Jan answered. She expected more cross-examination, but her aunt surprised her. Dropping the subject of Jan's whereabouts, she asked instead, "Have you eaten anything?"

As a matter of fact, Jan hadn't. She'd even forgotten about the food in her backpack. She muttered something about not having had time, and her aunt sighed in exasperation. "Between hospitals and everything else, you're too run-down to be skipping meals. Come in and eat

198

something." Aunt Leah led the way to the kitchen and started to get leftovers out of the fridge. "And the police. Jan, I don't know what you've been up to, I expect it's the same thing that made you pull that foolishness with all those pills, but the police were here twice today looking for you. Along with that Mr. Randall from the State Fire Inspector's Office. Is that why you hid all day?"

"I wasn't hiding," Jan mumbled. Her aunt met the lie with a sniff. Jan hurriedly changed the subject. "Is Andrea still up?"

"She's in her room," Aunt Leah said, starting the tea kettle. "Honestly, neither one of you has been behaving normally lately." Jan finished the warmed-over meal just as her aunt placed a mug of the herbal cure-all tea in front of her. "Drink that. Every drop of it, Jan. What with skipping meals and dodging the police—*and* trying to kill yourself and wandering around at night instead of staying in bed—you're going to ruin your health completely."

Yeah, killing myself would really ruin my health. Aunt Leah left her alone after she'd eaten, allowing Jan to go upstairs without further questioning. She knocked hesitantly on the door of Andrea's room.

"Go away!"

The response caught Jan off balance. She knocked again. "Andrea? I have to talk to you. Look, it's important."

"Tough."

Jan tried the door, but it was locked. After waiting fifteen minutes, knocking at intervals but getting no further response, Jan went into her own room. Her plan hadn't included this. Now what? She didn't want to hold a confrontation through a locked door.

She went over to the window and stared down the street toward the shadows under the Simpsons' elms. A gleam of streetlights reflecting off chrome was the only evidence that Mike was waiting down there in his car. Jan turned off the lights, flipping them on and off twice in the "okay" signal she'd arranged with Mike, then leaving them off. She didn't get undressed. It was going to be another long night, but if Andrea tried anything, Jan intended to be ready.

Time passed. Jan heard the clock downstairs chime midnight and counted the strokes. She couldn't quite . . . the numbers weren't coming out right in her mind. She started to giggle; this was silly, she could count! She'd learned how to count years ago. . . . She awoke again with a jerk, just as she started to doze off. She shouldn't be this sleepy. She had to stay awake.

She'd been drugged again. Jan stood up. If she could get to the window, call Mike . . . She took a step toward the window, swaying, then collapsed to her knees. She had to tell Mike . . . tell Mike . . .

As she slipped into unconsciousness, Jan realized she was the one who'd been trapped. Aunt Leah's tea . . .

THIRTEEN

Jan drifted in and out of consciousness. She was vaguely aware of a hand grasping her arm, forcing her down the stairs and out the back door, along the path. Her mind was lost in a nightmare of whispering voices. *Be careful, Jan . . . the tea. Something in the tea. Mike. Call Mike. Tell him . . .*

She stumbled slightly, waking up momentarily. The path. Why was she outside? A door was in front of her, one she recognized as the door to Aunt Leah's small workshop. She must be sleepwalking again. Funny, usually she woke up once she realized she was out of bed. But her mind didn't want to wake up this time.

Sleepwalking. Someone had used her sleepwalking to make her look crazy. Dreams melted

*into one another, as Jan heard her mother call-
ing once more, waking her up in time to get out,
waking her up at Julie's. . . . Jan could hear
her again now, calling. Maybe Mom was trying
to protect her from Andrea. It had to be Andrea,
Mike had figured it out.*

There were smells Jan recognized, paint and
thinner, linseed oil, scorched fabric. *Not gasoline. Not this time. There hadn't been any gas
the first time, just smoke, thick choking smoke,
choking her. . . .* Jan tried to open her eyes,
aware something was wrong. *Something wrong,
just like the first fire . . . all the fires. There'd
been so many fires. In the distance she heard a
whisper.* "Wake up, Jan, wake up. . . ."

*Fires. For a moment dream folded on dream
as Jan again saw her home wreathed in flames,
and the Blue Willow, and the school fire she'd
seen only in nightmares, and fire fighters surrounding the Rodgerses' house while she
watched from the shadows. Woven through the
flames of her dream was a dream of nightmare,
as two months of terror blended into a single
blaze and her mother screamed,* "Jan! Now!
Wake up!"

She woke up.

* * *

Blank canvases, her aunt's easel, and paint-smeared rags were piled around the electric heater in Aunt Leah's workroom. Several of the rags were smoldering, and there was a smell of scorched canvas. The heater was turned on high, and the protective metal grid had been pried off the front and rags jammed against the glowing element. As Jan fought to clear the sleep from her mind and overcome whatever had been in the tea, one of the smoldering rags burst into full flame. The fire spread quickly, catching the cotton curtains over the window and moving down the storage shelves toward the supply of thinners and linseed oil.

Jan struggled to get to her feet. Between the flammable chemicals and fabrics, the place was a death trap. She made it to her knees, when a violent shove knocked her back to the floor.

"No!" Andrea was screaming at her and pushing her back down. "Dammit, why didn't you stay asleep? Jan, no, I don't want to . . ." Tears were streaming down her cousin's cheeks, but that didn't stop her from taking a vicious swing at Jan's head with a board. Jan fell flat on her face, and the board passed inches above her head. As she rolled frantically to one side, Jan recognized the board as one of the homemade shelves lining the room. Andrea brought the clumsy weapon crashing down as Jan scrambled the other way. It hit Jan on the shoulder, sending pain shooting down her arm, but she managed to get to her knees. She sprawled sideways as Andrea, sobbing, kicked at her. One of the canvases, now burning, fell over beside Jan as she wriggled away from the flames.

"Jan, no, please, I have to, I *have* to!" Andrea grabbed Jan as she finally made it to her feet. By now her cousin was shrieking incoherently, a jumble of words that made no sense. Her strength was frightening. She held Jan in a death grip as fire spread around the room. Oily smoke filled the small area as Jan fought to free herself from Andrea's grasp. She was weak from whatever drug she'd been given, but she had to get away, out into the clean night air.

The heat grew more intense. Jan tried to pry Andrea's fingers loose. Andrea twisted around behind Jan, still clutching Jan's arms and making it impossible for Jan to hit her. Jan kicked backward as hard as she could, but to no effect. She started for the doorway. If she couldn't break away from Andrea, she'd pull them both to safety. As though realizing what Jan was trying to do, Andrea grabbed the end of a shelf.

The other end was already ablaze, and it tore away from the wall in a shower of sparks.

The flames ebbed momentarily as the door opened, letting in a draft of fresh air. Through the smoke Jan recognized Mike, and her efforts to escape doubled. Then the flames swirled higher, as oxygen fed the blaze. Mike lunged for the struggling pair and grabbed Jan's arm. "Let her go, Andrea!" he shouted. By this time the fire was making a hungry roar. Andrea didn't answer and didn't release her grip. Instead she tried to pull Jan closer to the wall, where the fire was most intense.

For a moment Jan felt like a wishbone, being ripped in two by Andrea and Mike. Then Mike reached past her, raising his arm and bringing his fist down like a club on Andrea's wrist.

She screamed, a high, thin sound that almost covered the crack as a bone broke under the impact. Her hands fell from Jan's arms, and Jan stumbled forward as Mike roughly pulled her out the door, into the dark night air. In the sudden chill, goose bumps rose on her arms. They fell to the ground, a few yards from the studio. Jan could hear sirens in the distance. This time she welcomed the sound.

Mike hauled himself up off the ground, gasping out, "Gotta get Andrea." Jan sat up, her head whirling. Andrea? She looked wildly around—her cousin was still inside the workshop. There was a crunching of gravel behind her as Mike added, "Take care of Jan, Mrs. Scott, I've got to get Andrea out!" He ran back to the studio and plunged into the flame-filled doorway.

"Take *care* of you?" Jan felt herself being pulled to her feet, as Aunt Leah grabbed her. "I've been trying to take care of you! For weeks! I wanted you to die with your parents. Damn you, why aren't you dead?"

As Aunt Leah pushed Jan back toward the studio and the fire, the last of the drug haze cleared from Jan's mind, and she recognized the low, vicious voice and the talonlike grip on her arm. Aunt Leah! Her herb tea had been a cover for drugs. She must have been helping Andrea all along. Desperate and fully awake now, Jan twisted in her aunt's hands and pulled her left arm free. She slipped on the dew-soaked grass, but managed to keep her feet. Striking left-handed, Jan hit Aunt Leah on the side of the face, but the awkward blow was too weak to stop the crazed woman. The twisted expression of hatred on her aunt's face didn't

207

alter as once more she tried to push Jan into the fire.

Jan's bare feet slipped again. She lost a few more inches, then Aunt Leah's hands fell away as Mike ran out of the studio, Andrea in his arms. The back of his sweatshirt was smoldering, and Andrea's clothes were on fire. He dumped her on the wet grass and rolled her over and over, extinguishing the flames, then dropped on his back, rubbing against the ground. Aunt Leah let out a cry and scrambled over to her daughter, dropping to the ground beside her. Jan stood there, forgotten for the moment. Andrea was unconscious—or dead— Jan couldn't tell. Then, with a fierce growl, Aunt Leah launched herself at Jan, her hands reaching out for Jan's throat. They fell backward together on the slippery lawn, Jan trying desperately to keep those hands, strengthened by mad rage, from her neck.

"Mrs. Scott!" Mike sat up and stared for an instant, and Jan realized he still hadn't caught on to her aunt's role in the night's events. Then he ran toward them. As he grabbed Aunt Leah from behind, the heat inside the burning studio passed the flash point, and the cans of turpentine stored in the closet caught. The small building exploded, the blast knocking all three of them to the ground. Moments later the first fire fighters reached them. As hoses were dragged across the flower beds, and lights came on all down the block, a paramedic ran up and knelt beside Andrea, checking her injuries. Shakily Jan got back on her feet. Mike joined her, slipping an arm around her waist as they watched the medic in silence. A few feet away, Aunt Leah lay on the ground sobbing with frustration and hate.

The next few days passed in a haze of lawyers, police, and doctors. Uncle Peter collapsed on the second day and was put in the hospital, suffering from shock. Shock didn't seem a strong enough term, Jan thought. Not for a man whose world had been destroyed.

Andrea was in the burns unit, a policeman seated outside her door. Jan visited her once, the hospital smells almost triggering panic, and had to listen to an incoherent, tear-choked confession. She'd already heard a less confused version from Inspector Randall. Aunt Leah was in jail, refusing to speak to anyone, including the lawyer Uncle Peter had hired. The only time she'd spoken, according to Mr. Randall, was when Uncle Peter had tried to visit her. She'd begged the jailers not to make her see him. That had been the point at which Uncle Peter had collapsed.

It would take a long time to clean up the wreckage of so many lives, but a start had been made. The Rodgerses, innocent bystanders caught in Aunt Leah's schemes, were living in a motel while their home was rebuilt. Julie was out of the hospital; she wouldn't be scarred as badly as Andrea, but she'd carry the marks of Aunt Leah's greed for the rest of her life. Jan was staying with Barb and her family temporarily, while Uncle Peter remained in the hospital. Jan hoped someday they'd be able to pull their shrunken family together again.

She said as much to Mike when, finally, she was able to have some time alone with him. The last fire in what the local paper was calling the Kenowa Arsons was three days in the past. They were in the living room of Barb's home.

"Family?" Mike shook his head. "Jan, you really think your uncle is ever going to want to think about his *family* again? His wife offs his own brother and tries to kill his niece as well, and even drags his daughter into it. . . . I don't think he'll blame you, but he sure won't ever be comfortable around you. I wouldn't be. Man, he doesn't have *anybody* left."

"He does have me," she answered in a low voice. She'd given a lot of thought to this in the past days. "And Andrea will get out of prison someday. She's still a minor, and she didn't do that much. Aunt Leah—well, she'll probably get a long sentence. Maybe life. I expect he'll get a divorce, eventually, after the trial and everything."

"All I've gotten so far has been bits and pieces of the story," Mike said. "I still don't understand what happened. Just that your aunt decided to kill your folks. Beyond that, I'm lost. Why'd she go after you, and how'd she get Andrea messed up in all of it?"

Jan sighed and leaned back against the sofa cushions. "I was supposed to have died with my parents in the first fire. That was the whole point, she wanted a clean sweep. Dad dead, Mom dead, me dead—and the business would have gone to Uncle Peter. And, more to the point, eventually to Andrea. The whole time, Aunt Leah was trying to grab an inheritance for Andrea.

"She put dead batteries in our smoke detectors, then started the fire." Jan shut her eyes, remembering. "Then I managed to get out. I inherited everything, not Uncle Peter. I think she must have come up with the new plan as soon as I moved in with them and started sleepwalking. The police have found six different doctors around, places like Springfield, Decatur, Champaign, who took her on as a new patient and gave her prescriptions for tranquilizers and sleeping pills, all sorts of different drugs. She's always used that horrible ginseng tea, so it was easy to dope me. And she kept upping the dose."

Wordlessly Mike stood up and left the room. When he returned, he had a couple of tall glasses of orange juice. He handed her one. "Speaking of which, remember what the doc told you. You need to get the rest of the junk out of your system."

Jan made a face; she was starting to hate juice. She was now in the hospital's outpatient detox program because of the prescription drugs she'd unwittingly become addicted to. She took a sip and went on.

"That's it, mostly. She didn't tell Andrea everything at first, just had her follow me when I walked in my sleep—*that* wasn't under her control—and tell me lies and type stuff on my computer. Andrea always pretty much did what Aunt Leah told her, and I think she convinced Andrea they could get me out of the way without hurting me. Aunt Leah did most of it; I think she started all the fires except the Blue Willow. That one was Andrea. She followed me from the party. But Aunt Leah was the one who stole your keys." Tears started as Jan said, "It wasn't until after she killed Mr. Kahn, because she was afraid he'd seen her, that she told Andrea everything."

"And after that Andrea helped her try to kill you, because she didn't want her mother arrested," Mike said quietly. "It just doesn't make sense."

"I don't think it can, to a normal person," Jan said. "Neither of them was thinking very straight. Murder must do that to you."

"Yeah." They sat quietly for several minutes, just thinking.

Barb stuck her head into the room. "Want me to do another disappearing act, or can I come in now?"

Mike shook himself, like someone waking up. "Hey, it's your house," he said.

Before long the rest of the Mitchells joined them, and the conversation shifted determinedly from fires and crime to a new movie playing downtown. Mike stayed a while longer, then excused himself. Jan walked him to the door, and they spent a long time saying good night. Mike was the only thing in her life that hadn't been lost or damaged in the past year. Somehow Jan knew he'd always be there.

She went back into the living room and let the conversation of this latest temporary family flow around her. Jan didn't know how long she'd be here. She was taking Mr. Kahn's last advice and repeating her senior year, but whether she'd stay with the Mitchells, or with Julie's family once their home was rebuilt, or whether she would join Uncle Peter in a new home, was up in the air.

After a while she said good night and went into the guest room. She lay awake on the unfamiliar mattress, staring up at the darkened ceiling. There was one thing she still hadn't told Mike, or the police or anyone else. Someday, she thought, she would tell Mike and possibly Uncle Peter, but it was her secret for now. She had finally relived all of that first fire in her dreams, and she knew now what had awakened her in time to escape. It was the same thing that had saved her at the Rodgerses' that night, and in the studio. A voice, calling to her.

She could hear it again, but this time it wasn't telling her to wake up. Instead Jan heard her mother saying, *"Rest, Jan. Rest. You can sleep now."*

She could sleep, without nightmares. And Jan knew she wouldn't walk in her dreams ever again.